Ted's Tales

Ted Delgrosso

PAGE PUBLISHING
Conneaut Lake, PA

First originally published by Page Publishing 2022

ISBN 978-1-6624-8399-8 (pbk)
ISBN 978-1-6624-8400-1 (digital)

Printed in the United States of America

Contents

——————— *Part 1* ———————

Contemporary Fiction

The Trick

MY GRANDFATHER WAS A great hunter. In his community, he was known to get a deer every year and was sought after for advice on hunting techniques and strategies. The walls in his living room, his dining room, and his workshop in the basement were all decorated with trophies. Many times, during our visits, he would serve wild game as supper, telling us what it was only after the meal was over.

As his grandchildren came of age, he would take us into the woods and teach us about the environment, the game animals, and the various hunting skills. Everything that had to do with the hunt was taught to us in a way that emphasized respect for nature and her beasts. We were taught how to dress for the woods in all seasons, how to move as quietly as possible, how to read the weather, and even how to render first aid for minor cuts and scrapes.

As we grew older, Grandpa gave us more specific lessons as they applied to a certain situation. He called these his *tricks*.

One such trick involved a situation where you are out on a deer hunt, and just as you are getting ready to shoot, the deer becomes aware of your presence and starts to run away. Already near the maximum range of your weapon, the deer will be gone in only a second or two. Rather than shoot at a moving target or give up, you try one last thing. In a loud voice, you shout out. Not necessarily a word or scream, but something in between. And maybe, just maybe, the deer will stop out of curiosity to look at whatever made that noise, thus giving you a last chance at a shot. The trick doesn't always work as no trick does, but once in a while, it will get you game.

I have since used Grandpa's tricks, and in a few situations, they have made the difference for me. And on one occasion it was a miracle.

I was in my early thirties and had made a name for myself as a hunter. I was fortunate enough to be able to afford hunts all over the world and had acquired quite a collection of trophies for my spacious den at home.

On one adventure, I was traveling by plane in Alaska near Nome on a polar bear hunt. I had hired a local professional pilot who knew the area by heart. The plan was to drop us down onto an ice field where he would then guide me on the hunt. As it turned out, about a half hour into the flight, the plane developed engine trouble.

The pilot made a few attempts to correct the situation to no avail, and finally, the engine just quit. He radioed a *Mayday* and our position. Then he focused on saving our lives. He kept the plane in a shallow dive, and things looked good as it appeared he would be able to glide the plane in for a controlled landing. But just as we prepared to touch down, a strong gust of wind hit the plane and slammed it into the ground.

It was the cold that woke me up. As I regained my senses, I realized that I had been thrown from the plane and survived the crash. As for the plane and pilot, both were gone. A diminishing fire atop a pile of debris was all that remained. I must have been out for a while because it appeared the fire had been burning for a long time. I searched for the pilot but discovered that he had perished. I could not yet even recover his body.

It was then that the truth of the matter hit me. I was alone with only the clothes on my back. I had been prepared for a one-day hunt, but that included supplies from the plane. Things like my pack, rifle, hell, and even my sidearm were now gone in the wreckage. I was alone with no food, water, or shelter of any kind. I wondered if there was anyone who had heard the pilot's Mayday. My life now seemed to depend on it. My only hope it seemed would be to wait for the fire to burn itself out and then to retrieve what I could to await rescue.

As I reviewed the situation, a flash of movement in the distance caught my eye. In an instant, all that had just happened to me was forgotten, for what I saw on the snow was no less than death. And it was heading my way.

At first, I nearly laughed at the irony of it. I had years upon years as a hunter and prevailed against some of the most dangerous predators. Lions, leopards, and even tigers had been challenged and defeated. And now, to end up like this. It was too much.

My death was closer now, obviously onto my scent. It had no idea that I was unarmed, as helpless as a baby seal before its lumbering presence. I was lunch, that's all—a cheap, easily-taken prey. As I looked upon it with awe and contempt, I knew I was a goner. My rifle, my pistol, those tools that made me superior, were all gone, ashes in the wreckage. As for the knife at my hip, a teaser that would only prove to be useless in the end.

I could see its breath now, coming in short and frequent bursts as it labored for its meal. All caution was gone now as it came toward me at almost a happy gait. I had minutes left to live, and I felt the sadness, the loneliness, and the fear all doomed men have faced.

Suddenly I remembered. I was not alone. My tools were not exhausted. I smiled as my plan solidified in my mind. Fear washed away and was replaced with determination. The polar bear was a scant hundred yards away now, and I could hear it snort as it breathed. It was a fearsome sight, but fear had left me. I had hope. It was time to try my plan. If it worked, I would survive. If not, well, I would not live long with my failure.

The bear was close now, and I focused not on it for a moment, but on myself. I calmed down as much as I could and slumped over to appear even weaker than I was. When I was ready, I again looked up at the bear.

It was very close now, only thirty yards distant. The bear had slowed to a careful walk, for it was cautious now. As it looked at me, it growled, checking to make sure there wouldn't be any surprises. I cast my eyes down to avoid direct eye contact but kept a close watch on the bear. It started a slow circle around me, and I pivoted as I had to keep the bear in front of me. I knew that I had only one chance at this, and if I was to survive the day, I would have to be exact in my timing. So I watched and waited.

Finally, now sure of himself, the bear once again ambled straight toward me. When it was about ten yards out, the bear stood up. I very nearly lost my plan to fear as I saw that this beast was almost seven feet tall. But I held together and didn't move. The bear dropped down and rushed me.

I made my move. The bear was certain of a meal now and reached out to get it. With all my strength, I raised myself out of the slump, spread my arms out as wide and high as I could, looked that bear right in the eyes, and screamed as loudly and as ferociously as I could.

The bear stopped in his tracks. It looked at me in a new way. I kept making growling sounds as I continued to glare at it. The bear gave out one last snort, turned, and walked away. I yelled again, and he actually ran away.

I stood there unmoving, watching the bear run away from an easy lunch. Easy? Not this guy. For I had put my heart and soul into becoming fearsome, and it had worked. That and what I said when I yelled. I yelled, "*Grandpa!*" Thanks, Grandpa.

Change

E MMET SET HIS COAT on the chair and switched on the kitchen light. It was cool in the house, and the little droplets of sweat hung on his forehead like balls of ice. He was scared. His home didn't even provide him with that old familiar security anymore, another drastic change. After catching his breath, Emmet walked into the bathroom and stared at the monster in the mirror. The murderer. The coward. How could he have done such a thing? The police must surely be looking for him now.

With an effort, Emmet turned from the mirror and walked into the bedroom where his wife, Cindy, lay, sleeping. He gazed down at her and noticed afresh how beautiful and peaceful she looked as she slept. "Nope, no problems here." He sat heavily on the bed and wiped his brow. Cindy slept on, oblivious to the one-character drama taking place next to her. "What can I do?" Emmet asked himself. "Call the police? Skip town? Clean off the car? What?"

It had all happened so quickly. He still felt the reeling numbness, but even more, he felt the weariness of impending dread. The deep-setting knowledge that all was over. Not only had he broken the law, he had also broken one of societies' most unforgiving taboos.

Emmet laid back on the bed, not bothering to remove his clothes or get under the covers.

In time, he settled down, and the reality of the situation became indistinct and then finally, was gone.

And so, for the last time as a free man, Emmet Powers, hit-and-run driver, slept.

A Letter to the Professor

DEAR PROFESSOR MICHAELS,

My name is Bob Karper. I am a student in your Creative Writing class. An incident occurred in your classroom yesterday that warrants an explanation.

I am a shooter, a pistoleer. Nothing threatening or illegal. It just means that my hobby is pistol shooting at a range. It is part of a very competitive sport that requires a lot of practice.

Usually, it has me at the range twice a week and on my hunt club property in rural New Jersey most weekends.

My favorite handgun is a Colt revolver. In a world of semiautomatic pistols, I still draw a few looks whenever I take out my old-style wheel gun from its case. It has a large heavy frame to handle the now ancient .357 magnum bullets, large blocky aiming sights, and real wood-checkered grips. I love it. As a model Trooper, it had its years of fame in the 1950s and 1960s as a favorite of law enforcement and criminals alike. But like other revolvers, it has given way to the more popular semiautomatic pistols in such calibers as the 40 caliber, the 45 caliber, and the ever popular 9 millimeter. But the Trooper Mark III is still one of my favorites, and it goes on many road trips with me.

Transporting a handgun in my state is quite complicated. There are lot of regulations that must be followed in order for you to remain legal. First off, the gun must be legally owned and registered. Then, it must be unloaded and placed in a sealed container of some sort. I use a gun case that resembles a plastic briefcase, complete with two-keyed locks and foam inserts to securely hold the revolver.

As for the ammunition, it must be kept secured in the vehicle away from the gun. The rationale behind this is to deny access to a loaded firearm. And when transporting the pistol, I am obligated to move it directly from my home to the destination and back again, no cruising around with a gun in the car.

And finally, it is understood if not mandated, that you would volunteer the fact that you have a firearm in the vehicle if the occasion arises where you are pulled over by police for any reason. The goal here of course is to avoid any misunderstanding in a potentially stressful environment. And since these rules are designed with public safety in mind, I've never had a problem with them. Over the years, I have put these guidelines into such practice that they have become second nature to me.

A few years back, I started to take my Colt to the range to practice my shooting skills. I even started reloading my own ammunition to keep the costs down. The unique characteristic of the .357 magnum is that, it is the same diameter as the less powerful but much cheaper .38 caliber cartridges. Both can be fired from the same gun. I ended up reloading and shooting the .38s most of the time, practicing with the .357s only rarely.

As time went on, I did relax somewhat in that I didn't always lock the gun case when I placed it in the car. It wasn't required by law, and the case never left my sight anyway. It was always the last thing I put into the car and the first thing out of it.

It was during these shooting years that I decided to attend college. As a United States Navy veteran, I was eligible for tuition assistance, so off I went. I wasn't sure what degree to pursue at the time, so I started out by taking general courses. And one such course, Professor Michaels, is the one you teach.

Although book bags are the style around campus these days, I cannot bring myself to place my course books in a backpack. I struggled for another solution. And then it occurred to me that my gun case, stripped of the foam inserts, would be a perfect way to bring my books and notepads to class. There was enough room for any other accessories I would need. So I developed a new routine. I would use the case to transport my books to class. Whenever I wanted to practice with the handgun, I would remove the books, load up the foam and the gun, and head off to either the range or the hunt club property. Upon my return, I would then lock the gun in the safe, remove the foam, and place my course books in the case. Simple, right?

And this brings me to yesterday. I was a little late getting up, and I had a story due for your class. Since I like to get to class a bit early, I quickly grabbed my case and drove to the college. It turned out that I was among the first few students to arrive in the classroom, so I had a few moments to relax. Finally, at your arrival, everyone stopped talking and took out their assignments. I opened my briefcase to take out the story. My Colt .357 magnum peeked back at me.

And so, Professor, that is why you saw me slam down the lid on my briefcase and run out of your class like a maniac yesterday morning. I do apologize for any distraction I may have caused, but under the circumstances, I am sure you understand. And I guarantee it will not happen again.

Your student, Bob Karper

PS I have decided to submit this account as my story assignment.

Master/Pet

TODAY WAS MY DAY off, and I was in bed this morning enjoying a few extra hours of sleep. Until, that is, I felt a couple of nudges by the dog's wet nose on my elbow. Shadow needed to go out.

So I got up, threw on some clothes, and went downstairs. Shadow was already at the back door. I opened the door, and out he ran. He did his business out in the yard, and I followed him out with the pooper scooper. Shadow started walking around the yard checking for signs of intrusions by the likes of squirrels and rabbits. As I, myself, now had an urgency to pee, I called him to go back inside. Shadow ignored my calls until he finished his *security check* but finally strolled back to the house.

When I came back from the bathroom, Shadow was waiting for me by his food bowl.

And so, I changed his water and started to prepare his breakfast.

Now Shadow eats only the best. My wife, Susan, shops each week for him and purchases fresh chicken and ground beef along with rice, barley, and sweet potatoes. Each weekend, she cooks all this up and then portions it out into meal-sized plastic baggies. And so, this morning, the routine was easy for me. A portion of barley, chicken, sweet potato, and a scoop of premium dry dog food were all blended in the bowl with a bit of hot water added. Shadow doesn't like cold food, so I mixed it all up and served it to him.

I watched him eat which didn't take too long. When he was done, Shadow rewarded me with a look, a few tail wags, and a burp. I felt good as I took his bowls to the sink to wash them.

When I was done, Shadow let me know he wanted to go back upstairs, so I opened the door. And up the stairs he went. I was feeling a bit tired myself, so I followed him up. By the time I reached the bedroom, Shadow had already taken my spot on the bed and was fast asleep, so I ended up dozing off in my wooden desk chair.

After all, Shadow is a good pet.

The Mermaid

In the deep woods.
One road to the world.
High atop a fog-shrouded mountain peak.
Hotel lamp a lonely sentinel on the outer porch.
And the wind…how it moaned, cried, screamed, and died.
The hotel was ours, ours for the night.
Twenty rooms it was, only two made up for us.
Us…we were eight, five in my party, three in theirs.
They all girls, we all boys.

The central room of the hotel had two forty-foot halls that extended
    like giant arms stretched out tight.
Two drearily furnished wings completed the symmetry of the first
    floor.
The huge central fireplace made it magnificent.
And the stairs…oh yeah!
Dark dismal shadows playing on the walls.
Creaky…of course.
The hallways were dark enough to be tunnels in the fragile light.
Giant spiders just beyond sight.
All in all, a frightful night, and me alone with strangers.

The upstairs was large, but it was a false place of long hallways and
    countless doors.
Our two were fifteen and sixteen, left, in front.
And there was a bathroom nearby, end of the hall.
But there was nothing to do up there, it threw you away.

The central room though grabbed us and turned us into the children
   we really were.

And it was fun!
Exploring that huge room made us all one with the hotel, guardian
   of the mountain.
The fireplace though looked like a huge gaping mouth.
I wasn't the only one to notice.
Compelling simply by its size.
Oddly immaculate, it had a perfect set of logs on its hearth as if it
   had been waiting.
Waiting? I thought. *Waiting for what?*

The rug, did I tell you about the rug?
It wasn't a carpet, oh no!
A carpet merely completes a furnished room.
A rug, this rug most of all, made the hotel a home!
Oval, it served as a transition from the cold hardwood floor to the
   promised warmth of the fireplace.
Just slightly thicker than you would expect.
The rug caressed the toes as you grazed through it.
It gave you up only after what seemed to be a firming of the grip.
As if it wanted to…keep you.

The mantelpiece was a mixture of old relics.
Deer antlers stuck out at odd angles.
A set from an antelope hung nearby. Then the owl. Pure gray with
   eyes of gold and black.
The eyes stared out with infinite alertness, infinite capacity.
The eyes of the owl challenged my very being.
An old urn sat in the center of it all.
Uncle Charlie, perhaps.
Or maybe the founder of this here fine hotel.
The urn tempted me to look inside it,
But I was not about to gaze upon the ashes.

Not on this night.

As the central room became more familiar, we relaxed.
Outside the fog roamed, the wind howled, but here we were safe.
Or were we.
The cards came out, soda and chips appeared.
The games began.
Thrust. Parry. Compromise.
Once we became one group, we all relaxed even more.
Conversations became more personal.
Tempers flared.
Laughter sprinkled the room.

I got up to explore one of the wings.
I was not alone…but, oh how I was.
The room was dark, lit mostly by the lamp outside.
The furniture in the room, shadows of dark that seemed to be…moving.
An old, old chair. A writing desk.

And then.
And then.
The mermaid.
A statue of wood it was. No seams.
Dark brown stain. One tone.
Seated on a rock near a wooden seashore.
Reclining really.
The tail, fine detail. The body, narrow and smooth.
The hair, the hair…my god, the face!

The evil scowl of a hag's face looked into and past my eyes, terrifying
    in its intensity, its lust.
The fragile case that enclosed the mermaid became a Pandora's box,
    and I prayed it would not open.
I turned away, afraid for my soul.
For I had seen a sight no living man should see.
The mermaid, the mermaid, pray never come for me.

The Sea Bat

T HERE ARE MANY WAYS that a new member of a club or other organization is initiated.

Some require the new member to pay special dues or perform a certain task. Most of the time, however, initiation means that members get a chance to play a trick on the new guy.

Thompson was sitting on the mess deck of the navy destroyer, talking with his new friends as they played a card game at one of the tables. Thompson was a new guy. He had only been on board for two weeks, and this was his first underway. The ship was at sea, and Thompson and his buddies were enjoying a few hours of time off.

"Say, Nessley, are we out far enough for sea bats?" asked Watson, looking up from his cards.

"We've been in sea bat country for the last six hours," replied Nessley. He was a navigator, so he knew about that kind of thing.

"What's a sea bat?" asked Thompson, taking the hook.

Banders smiled, almost giving it away, but Watson quickly spoke up.

"A sea bat is a creature that flies only at sea. It can be dangerous, especially to sailors out on deck at night. Didn't they tell you about them at school in boot camp?"

Thompson looked around. They were looking at him as if he was the dumbest person on earth.

"No, they didn't, but I did miss a few sessions," he said.

"Well, around here it's important to know about sea bats. They can be dangerous," said Banders.

Thompson looked at Banders. He wasn't sure he liked him yet because Banders was quick with a wisecrack. *But I guess it's all part of being new onboard*, Thompson thought. But then again, "How come I never heard of them?" he asked out loud, suspicion in his voice.

"Most people don't know about them," Banders answered. "Sea bats don't go near land, and it's only sailors that even see them and only rarely at that."

"It's a good thing too," added Watson.

"Why is that?" Thompson was curious now.

"Because sea bats are dangerous. Didn't you hear what Watson and Banders said before?" Nessley talked as if Thompson was a child.

"Listen here," he continued, "a sea bat is a kind of bat that feeds on fish and other things at night. It flies very quietly and is one of those things that is not afraid of people. But it isn't too big either, only about…what, three feet?" Nessley looked to Banders and Watson for confirmation.

"About a three-to-five-foot wingspan is what I heard," said Watson.

"Right," said Nessley. "Anyway, sea bats are the main reason why you keep your hat on when you go out on deck at night, or at least, keep your hair cut short. It's especially dangerous for lookouts because if they sleep on watch, the sea bat goes after them."

"What in the world are you talking about?" asked Thompson. He had heard some weird stories, but this was too much. Besides, he was in training to become a lookout.

"Well, a sea bat is always hungry," said Watson, taking up the story. "And it has very sharp claws on its feet. It will try to swoop down and grab you if it is hungry enough and if it thinks it has a chance at you. That's why you should never sleep on lookout watch. Those are the people who get attacked most often, but it could happen to anyone on deck at night."

"What is this about the hat and hair?" asked Thompson, now fully involved.

"There have been cases where sea bats actually lifted guys up off the deck a bit because they were able to get a grip on the guys' long hair. I don't know how true that is, but Clark over there said it happened just like that on his last ship."

Watson pointed to an older sailor, a boatswains' mate, seated at another table. Clark had a reputation as a grouch, especially with new guys, so Thompson decided not to go over and ask him about the sea bat.

The conversation died down for a while after that as the four sailors paid more attention to their card game. After about twenty minutes, Watson got up, said goodnight, and left.

Nessley was dealing a new hand a few minutes later when Watson came running back, all excited.

"Hey, you guys. Come on," he said, breathing hard. "I think somebody caught a sea bat on the fantail."

Thompson started to say something but noticed that Banders and Nessley had already stood up and were running for the door with Watson.

"Hey, wait up," he shouted, running after them.

Somehow, as everyone was running to the back of the ship, Thompson found himself in the lead. As he got closer to the fantail, he noticed a large box on the deck with a small crowd of sailors standing around. Batsel, the aft lookout, was talking excitedly. His headphone set was off his head and down around his neck.

"The thing was flying around me and just landed on the edge of the open box here. So I pushed it in and slammed the lid down right on top of it. It's in there," Batsel said, pointing to the box.

Thompson looked at the box. There wasn't any movement, but he was full of curiosity and had to look. He bent over quietly and gently picked up the lid. He peered into the box, expecting to see the sea bat. Instead, he found himself looking at a sign that said, *Welcome Aboard*. Thompson was just starting to realize what everything had been about when the New Guy Ceremonial Paddle, swung enthusiastically by Banders, hit him hard, right on the rump.

A Tale for Christmas

YEARS AGO, BEFORE HOUSING developments and everything that goes along with them pushed the woods back, many people in my town would trek out to the rural areas during the holiday season and cut their own Christmas tree down. There was much more public land in those days, and most authorities turned a blind eye to the activity as long as you weren't too obvious about it.

My dad packed Jimmy and I into the station wagon. It was a cold night five days before Christmas, and we were going to the country to get our own tree.

"Take your hats and gloves off when the heat comes on," said Dad as we started off down the street. "Unzip your coats a little too."

"Why should we do that?" asked Jimmy, my younger brother.

"Well, if you leave all your winter clothes on when it gets warm in the car, you will sweat," Dad answered. "Besides, when we go out into the cold later, you can put on the hat and gloves, and they will help you stay warm."

Dad was so smart.

The drive out to the country took about forty-five minutes. Jimmy and I were just starting to get restless when Dad pulled over.

"Okay, here we are," he said, reaching behind the seat to get the flashlight and the camping saw. "Zip up, put on your hats and gloves, and let's go."

After checking us out, Dad led the way up the low hill next to our station wagon. My boots felt a little heavy, and in the deep snow, I was moving slowly. Luckily, so was Dad.

"Keep an eye on your brother, Ted," he said. Dad had arranged the hike where he took the lead, followed by Jimmy, then finally, me. This way, Jimmy and I could follow in his footsteps, and no one would fall behind. Even though it was nighttime, the bright snow on the ground helped us to see in the dark. Dad had his flashlight just in case.

At the top of the hill, I saw a pine tree and said, "How about this one, Dad?"

He looked it over and replied, "No, see how crooked the trunk is? Let's keep on looking."

We moved on. The land flattened out a little, which was nice because I was getting tired from climbing the hill. Jimmy must have been tired, too, but he didn't say anything. So I didn't either. As we walked on, I noticed several pine trees off to our left. I thought we should head over to them, but it was Jimmy who said, "Wow, look at this one!"

The tree he was pointing to was straight as an arrow and covered with layers of beautiful pine needles. I felt a sudden twinge of jealousy because Jimmy had picked this tree, but I relaxed and agreed.

"This is a great tree, Dad. What do you think?"

"Well," Dad replied, stroking his chin, "it does look pretty straight but wait a minute. How are we going to get this monster into our living room?"

He was right. As I looked again, I realized that this huge tree was too big to fit in our house.

"Told you, Jimmy," I said.
"Did not," he shot back.
"Knock it off, you two," said Dad. "And let's keep going."

As we passed through the grove of huge pine trees, the land started up again. *Oh no*, I thought, *not another hill.*

Sure enough, this hill proved to be even steeper than the last one. I was just about to complain to Dad when I saw him look up and point to a tree on the hilltop.

"Look at that, fellas," he said. "Let's go."

We just about ran up the hill toward that beautiful tree. As I approached, I went through my Christmas tree checklist:

Straight trunk, yes.

Small enough to fit in the living room, yes.

This is it, then.

We stopped, unconsciously surrounding the tree. Dad was just about finished looking it over when he frowned.

"What's wrong, Dad?" asked my brother.

"We can't take this tree, guys," he said.

"Oh, why not?" I groaned, tired and cold.

"Look at it carefully, and you tell me," he responded.

When I went around to his side, I saw what he meant. About two thirds up the tree was a small squirrel's nest. Dad was right. We couldn't take an occupied tree.

"See the squirrel's nest?" I said to Jimmy. "We can't take this home, can we?"

"No, I guess not," answered my brother.

"Well then, let's start over again," I said, feeling a little better.

Since we were at the top of the hill, we could see a fair distance around us. Dad quickly spotted another tree, and off we went.

The tree looked good as we got closer to it. Nice and straight, small enough to fit in the house and not a nest in sight. We took a second, closer look, then Dad said those magic words, "Okay, guys, this is it."

We stood back as Dad knelt down, found a spot for the saw, and started cutting. The tree came down quickly, and as it did, Jimmy and I yelled the traditional *Timber!*

I was just feeling good about things when I noticed that Jimmy was crying. "I want to go home," he said. "I want to go now."

I knew then as tired as I was, Jimmy must be feeling even worse. And when he ran out of steam, he could be very stubborn.

"Well, Jimmy, now that we have the tree, all we have to do is walk out with it," Dad said, hoping to salvage the situation.

Jimmy would have none of that.

"No, Daddy. I want you to carry me. I'm cold," said my brother.

I really couldn't blame him. We had been through quite an ordeal, and he was three years younger than I was.

I could see my dad thinking. He was going over his choices. I didn't think that even he could carry both Jimmy and the tree all at once. As for me, I couldn't carry anything, except for maybe, the saw.

"All right, listen up," said Dad, taking charge. "Jimmy, stop your crying, I will carry you out. Teddy, take the saw, be careful with it. Carry it with the saw blade teeth out like I taught you, and lead the way to the car. Just follow our tracks out, okay? Then I will come back and get the tree." He picked Jimmy up, gave him a quick hug, and said, "How does that sound?"

"Hmm," said Jimmy. And we started back.

The trip back to the car was one of silence. Jimmy muttered a few times, but Dad didn't speak. Even though I was tired, I felt that I wanted to ask Dad if I could return with him later to get the tree.

Back at the car, Dad got Jimmy onto the back seat and opened his thermos bottle.

"Here's a treat, guys," he smiled as he poured both of us a cup of hot cocoa. "Don't drink it too fast now."

Dad then covered Jimmy with a blanket and turned the car on to warm it up. After several minutes with the heater on, Dad turned the car off and put the keys in his pocket. He turned to us and said, "Okay now. It will be warm in the car for you two until I return with the tree. Wait here for me."

"Dad, can I go too?" I said. "I feel better now."

"Well, I will leave that up to Jimmy," Dad said. I hated when he did that.

"It's okay," Jimmy said slowly.

"All right!" I yelled, getting out of the car. "Come on, Dad, let's go."

After checking on my brother one more time, Dad joined me on the hike to get the tree. It wasn't bad. For one thing, I knew just how long it would take. And for another, the earlier tracks in the snow made traveling much easier.

We were just starting to climb the last hill when Dad motioned to me to stop. "What is it?" I whispered.

"Shh. Listen," he replied, quietly.

At first, I heard nothing. Then, I heard what sounded like deer running. And finally, I heard, clear as a bell, a deep voice that said, "Ho! Ho! Ho!"

Quickly, we ran up the hill. As we reached the top, we looked at where the tree was supposed to be, but it was not there. There was a small pile of sawdust but no tree.

When we got a little closer, Dad pointed and said, "Ted, look at that."

On the ground, about six feet from the tree stump, were two straight parallel lines in the snow. Between them were a bunch of deer tracks as if a small herd had stood there stomping the ground. Then, about thirty feet away, all the tracks and lines disappeared.

Dad and I both looked skyward without speaking. *No, it couldn't be*, I thought. *But what else then?* I thought back.

24

To this day, I don't know exactly what happened. Dad and I returned to the car and found Jimmy sleeping safe and sound. We stopped on the way home and bought a tree for *too much money* according to Dad, and we didn't tell Mom about what happened in the woods until Christmas Day. She didn't believe us anyway.

On Christmas morning, however, the oddest thing of all happened. A mysterious Christmas card, very large and in a red and green envelope, appeared beneath the last gift box under the tree. It showed a picture of Santa loading a pine tree onto his sleigh with the reindeer all lined up and ready to go. The woods in the background looked very familiar.

As for the message on the card, it said simply, "Ho! Ho! Ho!"

Morning Hunt

EARLY MORNING. COMPLETE DARKNESS replaced by just a hint of light from the eastern horizon. It was much darker looking down into the woods. Some silhouettes were appearing before my eyes but very little detail. I checked the grip on my crossbow because I knew the best time of the hunter's day was approaching.

As if on cue, I heard a soft rustling that told me a deer had stood up to my right. The light had started to come in a little better, but it was still too soon to shoot. The rustling sounds increased as other deer arose for the day. The sounds told me of movement nearby, but nothing had become visible yet. At that point, my strategy was to remain undetected, rely on stealth, control my breathing, minimize movement and sound, and hope my scent blocker would work to keep my human odor hidden.

More light now, and the silhouettes became sharper and with more depth. Trees, shrubs, and a general layout of the area became visible. No color yet, but my eyes could take over as my dominant sense. The rustling on my right was sporadic as the deer were in no hurry. I was calm because I was between them and the field, so I knew they would eventually pass me on their way to feed.

A few minutes later, color was added as the dawn approached. I was finally able to see the deer. Three, no four. All doe, but that's okay. It was early season, and I was after meat, not a trophy. A doe would do just fine. After a few minutes, they began to move toward the field. As they approached, I selected the one I wanted, the last one in the line, a large animal at least two years old.

But it was not to be easy for me. As I brought my crossbow up to take aim, the deer in front of my doe noticed the movement and stopped. She stomped her forward leg, and they all stopped. The heads came up. The ears twitched in all directions, and they all started to look around.

Things got serious at that point. The tables had turned. Now they were hunting me. Four animals with superior senses of sight, smell, and especially hearing were all trying to find me.

And if any one of them did, well, game over.

Time froze as I focused on stillness. My crossbow was not yet in position for a shot, and my only chance was to wait things out until the deer, all four of them, relaxed and resumed their journey to the field.

Seconds became minutes and minutes seemingly hours as I remained frozen in a position I had not selected. My muscles started to stiffen and then ache. I momentarily reflected on buying this crossbow with it being a lightweight model being the most important factor in the purchase. It was helping now, but I knew I could not last too much longer in this position.

I could start to feel my heartbeat as I grew more fatigued. I focused on the deer below me. Each time a pair of eyes swept over me, I had a moment of worry and then relief as they continued past. The deer seemed to relax a bit as the intensity of their search diminished.

Finally, I had my chance. The lead doe started off again past my tree stand. The others followed in a slow meandering way. They remained cautious as one by one they passed through my kill zone, but there was no more foot stomping. After a few more long seconds, the last doe got to where I wanted her to be.

And the rest was fairly easy. The crossbow was sighted in at thirty yards, and the shot was only slightly longer than that. I grunted to stop the doe, and once she was motionless and broadside, I released the bolt. It was a good hit, and my doe only traveled about forty yards before she collapsed.

The others had scattered at the sound of the hit, but that didn't matter. The day was mine, and I had the feeling of success not too often felt by deer hunters as the odds go. And so, as I climbed down the tree stand ladder, my thoughts turned to the next phase of the hunt. I still had to tag the deer and report it to the state wildlife authorities, by phone these days. Then I must field dress the deer, drag it out to my truck, and get it to the butcher. More work indeed, but a labor of love for this old hunter.

The Shot

THE ARROW ARCHED UP into the air, a perfect launch. I knew it was a hit the moment I released. The buck was a nice one. It did not jump at the sound of the arrow release but stood still as the arrow sped on. It was a forty-six-yard shot, so I had a few moments of thoughtful anticipation as the scene played out.

I had been deer hunting for most of my life. The wall in my studio at home displayed a few of the better deer, and I had enjoyed years of full freezers in the basement. I am a rather good cook, but my specialties are always venison preparations.

The bow represented the latest technology with more accessories than some cars, the best I could afford. It was as comfortable in my hand as a custom-made glove. The arrows were a combination of razor sharp broadheads, thin carbon shafts, and even illuminated nocks to track their progress.

As for skill, I was at the top of my game—archery lessons throughout my childhood, time placed aside through high school, college, marriage, and two children to practice, practice, practice. I was able to hit bull's-eyes from elevated stands of various heights as well as from ground level.

My camo gear, I had spent a small fortune for a set that was waterproof, windproof, silent, and infused with the latest scent absorber technology. My tree stand was a custom-built platform set up along the best deer run on the property. And all for this day, this deer, this moment...

I missed.

The Last Day

A S I WOKE UP, I knew not to move. My training was the first thing to come back to me, and I remembered the protocols. First, don't assume you are safe. The danger might still be present. So do your self-check as soon as you can, but assess the situation first. Okay then. I didn't hear or smell anything threatening. Through my slitted eyes, I cannot see any immediate danger. It was still daylight, and I was in the same area I remember prior to the explosion.

Next to check if I am all here and all right. Flex the toes, ankles, and legs. So far, so good. Next the fingers, hands, and arms. Uh-oh, my right arm seemed a bit stiff just above the elbow. The back, neck, and face, they seemed all right. I slowly moved my head, first left and then right, slowly, to check my surroundings. I seemed to be alone, so I went back to my arm. As I tried to raise it, I felt a sharp pain in my bicep, harsh but not a bone injury. I considered taking a look, knowing that if the enemy was nearby, my movement would attract attention, but deciding it was worth the risk.

Sure enough, blood was leaking out of my right bicep by now not too bad. But in the center was a nasty piece of shrapnel that went straight through my arm. Then the pain hit. I almost laughed at the irony (*you shouldn't have looked*) that the pain showed up only after I saw the wound. Okay, I can deal with it.

Next, I rolled to my left side and started to get up. I was stiff but able to sit up without too much difficulty. My weapon was close by and seemed intact. I continued the odyssey to my feet and though dizzy for a moment, was able to stand.

The mine had exploded along the trail as it curved to the right and up ahead of me. The fact that the center of the explosion was a bit uphill probably saved my life. Poor Jenkins, our point man wasn't so lucky. He had taken most of the blast and was literally blown to bits—pieces all over. Montague too was gone, hit by way too many bits of shrapnel. My mind took in the horror but quickly suppressed it as I bent to retrieve my M-16.

If there was to be a follow-on attack, it would have either happened by now (in which case, we would all be dead) or it was coming soon. Palistrant, Hoernke, Palmer, and I instinctively went back-to-back, setting a perimeter of sorts. Thank God my rifle was light enough to be handled with one hand as my right arm was useless. After what seemed like forever with no incoming, we started to relax. Hoernke noticed I was still bleeding at the same time I started getting dizzy again as my pain come back, more intense than ever. I started to slump down. Hoernke caught me and helped me down to the ground again. As he started to tend my wound, I could hear Palmer calling for the medivac. Then everything faded away.

I woke up in the chopper. The wind tore at my left side, but I felt it only through a haze. The medic must have given me morphine because there was no pain, only a feeling of dream walking. Hoernke was sitting behind me, his boots near my head. The others were there too. The door gunner was relaxed, so we must have been high up. I was as close to being at peace as I could ever remember being, and with that, I once again drifted off.

That was almost fifty years ago. It was indeed my last helicopter ride. That arm wound was serious enough to be my *golden bullet*, my magic ticket home. It was the early end of my second tour, and at the time, believe it or not, I felt a bit disappointed.

I still can't help but believe I had a bit of a death wish back then. Most guys doing two or more tours in those days were there mainly because the world had gotten too weird when they got home the first time. It sounds crazy, and, in a way, it is crazy. But there are those who know what I mean.

Anyway, as I sit here in my tree stand, the memory of my last day in the field in Vietnam still brings intense feelings. And like many, I have developed strategies for dealing with it all. I am still attracted to the woods and have spent most of my life as a hunter. But I hunt only deer now, not men. And to be honest, I don't even care anymore whether the deer show up.

Safe

Jason

T HE NIGHT WEATHER OUTSIDE was windy and stormy. I was in one of the safe houses but didn't feel so safe. They are after me. And they are good, curse them, so very good. My security detail in Baltimore was quickly overwhelmed. All were killed, and I barely escaped myself.

Thank God for Myra. She's sitting in the front room now, mini-Uzi at the ready, no doubt, on watch, my protector—the only one left.

It all started innocently enough, barely four months ago. I work for an export company, mostly legal—mostly that is. On occasion, the CIA or other agency tasks us with shipping weapons under the guise of medical equipment. No big deal. I'm sure we are but one of many companies across the nation to do such things. I oversee these operations.

Usually, these things go off without a hitch, and no one notices. Supply shipments occur every day, all around the world. But a few months ago, word started going around that some of these medical equipment shipments were being diverted, going to places not authorized by our government. As a matter of fact, it became known that these shipments were ended up being used by the opposition against our troops in the Middle East. Someone on the inside of things was betraying our country in a very direct and deadly way. And so, housecleaning was the result.

What gets me is that I don't know if I am targeted as a traitor. I don't feel like a traitor. I just did what I was told like I had always done. I had found out early on in this business that being in charge sometimes meant looking the other way and allowing others to make decisions. But I never expected this. As far as I know there is no warrant out against me. No way I can just turn myself in. It's too late for that now anyway. Baltimore showed me that.

And so I ran. I felt safe with Myra. Tomorrow, she will meet with an extraction team and take me to someone somewhere who will give me a new identity, a crash course in who I am to become and a plane ticket to yet another safe house where I can start over. It's not what I would have chosen, but it's better than what my bodyguards got earlier this evening.

Now I hear Myra in the other room. It sounds like she has opened the door. I can hear that the storm has quieted down a bit. I also hear something else, people coming in. At least three of them. Hushed voices. Maybe it's my extraction team coming to take me to the forger. They are early.

As I wipe the sleep from my eyes, the other possibility enters my mind. Maybe these guys are housecleaning. My door opens, and I see shadows in the dark.

* * * * *

Myra

I'm so tired of this crap. I used to be one of the heroes, the good guys. I served eleven years in the Army, one of the first women to make it through ranger training and then overseas for some real ass kicking operations, from Africa to Afghanistan, Colombia to Thailand, just to name a few. My being a woman only served to increase my value not only as a weapons' operator but as an undercover asset as well.

Then the fiasco in Tunisia. I was too quick on the trigger that day, and several civilians were killed. They told me that, though I was lucky not to get thrown into prison, my Army career was over. I was allowed to resign my commission and place myself back into the civilian world.

But that didn't last long. I got recruited by an outfit called FEOP, short for Feral Operations, a private security firm that would put my special talents back to work. It sounded good. The money was great, so off I went.

It was good to be back in action. My secret life quickly became my only life, and my cover as an international sales representative for a large communication company served me well when I *disappeared* for weeks or months on end.

Then for some reason, the work slowed down and became less intense and finally a little boring. I was only rarely attached to an action team. Most of my work became serving as a bodyguard for this or that important person. Most of the time, the threat level was low and slow, but there were occasional high intensity moments when one of the clients came under attack.

Things like that force you to stay sharp and always have a large variety of assets.

We at FEOP had safe houses, access to things like weapons, cash, cars, and caches of emergency equipment like passports, alternate IDs, plane tickets, and the like. And as an independent contractor, I always had access to all these things, no questions asked.

It all sounded great, and it was great for quite a while. But as the years went by, I grew less and less excited about the whole thing. I took myself out of team operations entirely and only accepted solo jobs. Even that didn't help, and I started to resent the fact that I was constantly putting my life on the line for causes and people I didn't really care about. I started thinking about getting out.

But getting out of such groups as FEOP isn't as easy as one would expect. Unlike the military, where you are bound by The Uniform Code of Military Justice and standards of classification, civilian outfits are a bit looser, especially with those of an *Independent Contractor* status. By granting such a status, these companies can maintain a degree of what is known as *plausible deniability* in case things get out of hand, something the military cannot do. And that is a double-edged sword for people like me. If I leave, I still maintain access to many assets. They cannot simply be switched off. But as FEOP administrators know this, they don't like giving up control of their personnel just because one decides to resign. And the nondisclosure contracts we all sign upon recruitment were laughable in real life.

Which brings me to this job here. I've been with Jason for a while now. His position always required team coverage, and I never had a problem working with them. But my contract as Jason's bodyguard is in addition to all that, a very smart move on his part. It certainly saved his life in Baltimore.

The way it went down was almost as I expected. I usually work independently from a bodyguard team as a redundant asset. I hang back, wait, and watch as the team takes the lead in the bodyguard duties. Though they know I am there, the team generally ignores me unless something bad happens.

On this occasion, however, they couldn't notify me of anything. The attacking crew was so good, so fast, that Jason's team was taken out in the first few seconds of the attack. My reaction was swift, but I barely got Jason and myself out of there in time. The smoke I threw as we ran down the alley was probably what saved us both. In actuality, it was a signal that I had him.

In all fairness, by the time the actual attack had occurred, I had already betrayed Jason. I knew enough of his situation by then to know that his position was untenable and that the assassination team would never give up until he was dead. And me? Totally expendable, simply by association. And so, I knew I had to negotiate myself away from Jason.

That is why I did two things prior to the Baltimore operation.

First off, I knew all about the attack. The team leader himself was an old acquaintance of mine (in this business you have acquaintances, not friends). He had contacted me a week before and warned me of the where and when. He even gave me the suggestion to *take the night off* in exchange for being taken off the hit list, at least temporarily.

I laughed and proceeded with my own counteroffer. It involved letting me rescue Jason on attack night to maintain credibility and then allowing me to take him to a safe house. Of course, he, team leader Mike, would know the safe house location. He would then wait a few hours for things to settle down. At that time, I would send him a signal, and he and his team could come to the house unopposed. In exchange, I would be allowed to walk away from the safe house, from the life, from everything. I would be safe. As for the second thing, I told Mike he was to report me killed in the raid as well as Jason.

I knew I was asking a lot of Mike, but after a moment of thought, he agreed. And so I brought Jason to the safe house.

* * * * *

Mike

The most difficult part of the job is the wait. Once our mission was completed in Baltimore, we quickly left the scene and reassembled at the warehouse. Jason had escaped with Myra, but we all knew that was part of the plan. If it turned out that any of Jason's bodyguard team had survived or if there were any surprise witnesses, we would be covered, especially Myra. Up to this point, our assignment to kill Jason and all his bodyguards was a failure. But the night was young.

And now for the waiting. We had agreed that Myra would bring Jason to the safe house in Woodlawn and allow him to calm down a bit before calling us in. Once the job was completed, we were to let Myra go, take the body with us, and sanitize the house. Just another day at work.

The team I lead is one of a few assets that the government keeps around for the nasty business that sometimes needs to be done.

Government involvement is never discussed, but we all know who pays the bills. We are well supported with, some say, *infinity at our disposal.* To help us accomplish our tasks, we are backed up with everything from intelligence assets, technical support from plumbers to drone surveillance, and an unlimited operational budget.

Where I come in is to ensure that my guys and gals are the best trained and best equipped team out there, fully capable of over-whelming any and all opposing forces. And that is not as easy as it sounds. You see, every mission is different. Assassination is our overall business, but the devil is in the details. The how, when, and where are the variables that drive our particular training methods for a specific assignment. We don't care about who or why.

Most of my team members come from the military in that they bring a boatload of capability with them at the outset. What I do is to upgrade their training to include all the latest technological advances. From the newest knives to the latest in form fitting body armor, my guys get it first. The evolution of killing technology has always been a top priority of civilization, a sad fact but true. It is a full-time job for many people to enable us to constantly be at the top of the pyramid.

Once we got the signal from Myra, we split the group in two and drove to the house. Wilkerson, Ellis, and Alameda formed a con-tainment perimeter around the house, and I led Marino and Cusack to the door. As expected, Myra let us in, Uzi in hand but not a threat. All was set, and as we entered the back room, Jason arose from the bed where he had been resting. He actually asked us if we were the extraction team.

"In a way," said Marino as he shot him twice in the chest. He was assigned the wet work for this evening.

Next was Myra. She smiled in relief thinking that all was over, and she would now be free to start a new life. That too was true in a way. Poor Myra. You see, in my business, at this level, there are never any loose ends allowed. It wouldn't be safe. And so, I felt a twinge of regret as Marino took her down.

The rest was just another part of the business, the cleanup. There was nothing in the way of blood contamination. In both cases, the bodies were quickly grabbed and turned face up even as they fell to the floor. And of course, the frangible bullets broke open soon after they entered, so there were no exit wounds. All the brass was recovered. And finally, they were both bagged within seconds.

All in all, we were at the house for less than fifteen minutes. As these things go, I'd say this was a well-executed operation with nothing notable about it.

Except for Myra.

I never knew this Jason fellow, but I had worked with Myra in the past. She will haunt me. At least for a little while.

Paintball Hero

REMEMBER THE FIRST TIME I went paintballing. It was somewhere back in the 1980s, and I was at Paintball USA in Newburg, New York. My friend's brother was having his bachelor's party at a paintball facility, pretty cool.

We had all paid our entrance fee and were issued our specialized gear for the games. We then milled about waiting for the buses that would take us all to the gaming areas. We were by then all dressed in our camouflage overalls, facemasks, helmets, and goggles, and each of us had a paintball gun.

In those days, the paintball guns were of the pump-action design, that is, you had to pump a slide under the barrel first toward you and then away in order to load a single paintball. Once you pulled the trigger and sent the paintball on its way, you had to pump the slide again to reload. Propulsion was provided by a compressed gas cylinder attached atop the gun.

I noticed a small range off to the side of our waiting area, so I went over to take a few practice shots.

It was a simple set up, just a piece of wood on the ground denoting the line of fire and about twenty feet away were the targets—three human-shaped plywood cutouts, each painted green.

As I didn't have much time, I decided to go for broke. As fast as I could, I rapid fired three shots, one at the head of each of the three targets. I scored three hits, three perfect bull's-eyes.

Now I had never picked up a paintball gun before. I had no skills, no practice on things like gun handling, trigger control, ammunition ballistics, or aiming techniques, things normally associated with range shooting. And yet, on my first outing, I scored three bull's-eyes. For that moment, I was the luckiest man alive. I knew it.

I then looked down to my left as a movement attracted my eyes. And there stood a little boy, no more than eight years old. He must have been one of the owner's kids or something.

There he stood, eyes wide and mouth agape. It was clear that he had never seen any shooting like that before and was amazed.

Did I tell him I was not a skilled shooter? That I had no idea what I was doing? That it was nothing more than beginners' luck?

Nah!

Before he could say, "Do it again," I gave that little boy a hero's wink and a nod and slowly walked off, just like in the movies.

Ro Li Revisited

AS I APPROACHED THE turnoff to what turned out to be Demarest Road, the feelings of uneasiness were replaced suddenly with clarity, certainty…I was back.

Within moments of the turnoff, I gazed to the right and saw the clearing where the Indian ceremonies had taken place, overgrown yes, but plain as day to me. Was that a shadowy figure near the tree? An Indian? No, just shadows and swaying branches.

Just a bit further down the road, I received a wonderful sight, the volleyball court, nearly intact. It seemed a beacon, an asphalt platform raised on a stony foundation surrounded by the same high fence I remembered, the gate ajar as it always had been, the net drooping but still there, a monument of the past.

Next to the volleyball court was the driveway, now blocked off with a length of wire rope that led down past the still standing infirmary, there just on the left. Beyond that lay, nothing, nothing but trees, bushes, grass, and trash—a place long overgrown, dumped upon, and forgotten. Forgotten? Not on this day.

I drove on hoping for more evidence, but Camp Ro Li, a summer camp for children, established and funded by our town's Rotary and Lions Clubs, had never really revealed itself to those on the road. I drove on though and after passing a few houses, turned around and headed back. An elderly couple in a blue sedan moved to pass me, and I flagged them down.

"Excuse me," I said, "but years ago there was a camp here. Camp Ro Li. Do you remember it?"

"Yes," the man replied, "I do. It is just ahead, what's left of it that is."

"Thank you," I said. "Say, do you think anyone would mind if I pulled in and walked around a bit?"

"No, I don't think so," answered the man softly with a smile. We parted, and I drove back the way I had come, back to Ro Li.

I pulled over next to the barrier on the driveway near the volley-ball court. As I walked around to get David, I spotted a box turtle on the roadside. After showing it to David, I placed the turtle in the car, then set off with my son to visit Ro Li.

We looked at the volleyball court but went past it. Shortly after on the left stood the infirmary building, now an old abandoned tiny house. The door lay inside where it had been kicked in some years back, the windows of course, held no glass, and the left side of the roof was agape with huge holes. I saw tidy rooms and shiny tables and comfortable chairs and heard our nurse humming as she attended a skinned knee, bloody nose, homesick camper. I blinked and saw the spiders, the ruins—the ghosts had gone.

David and I made our way on down the driveway and started off to the left, toward the main lodge and the cabins. Trees and grass stood in our path but not a building stood. A clearing with twen-ty-foot trees and thick shrubs stood where once our lodge/dining hall had been with its magnificent front porch. As we walked past this area, a small footpath, clearly defined, headed off to the right, down the hill toward the lake. It was nothing like the eight-foot wide, log bordered, stretched pathway we used to charge down on our way to the docks and swimming area. This path arched too far to the right, but it beckoned nonetheless. And down it, David and I went. He perched atop my shoulders.

The path ended abruptly at the lake. While I noticed a vaguely familiar general layout, it was nothing like the Ro Li shoreline of the past. Totally overgrown, this shore had no wide expanse of sandy beach, no aluminum docks for our skiffs and canoes, and no H-shaped swimming docks nor the floating raft that drew us out into the lake. The one thing that remained as it was a clearing, a patch of open, grassy shoreline on the other side of the lake. It was where we would show ourselves during the overnight hike around the lake before going uphill, a place for a last wave to those left behind at camp.

David and I went back up the trail to the central clearing. Off to the right was the area where the ten eight-person cabins had stood. Only a few boards now littered the ground, but the rocky slope that had been behind the cabins held familiar shapes for me. At one point, I saw the foundation of what our open-air wash station had been. I could still see the large white sinks, our towels hanging precariously on the edges, and water fights every morning. Aah! But only the cement floor stood before me now.

As David and I returned to the area near the infirmary, I saw the most significant thing from my past. I had totally missed it on the way in, but now it showed itself before me in all its former splendor.

The tetherball pole stood before me as it did all those years ago. The ball and rope were gone of course, but next to the pole on the asphalt at its base still extended the white line that defined one players' side from the other. It was then that David said, "Daddy, why are you crying?" For him, seeing his dad staring at a pole with tears in his eyes must have been a curious thing. I understood but how to explain? A smile and pat on the head were all I could offer, and he, at three, was yet wise enough not to push any further.

I made one more excursion, this to the site where our trading post, archery cabin and girl counselors' cabins had stood. Totally overgrown, here I saw evidence of the demolition that had occurred. Great mounds of dirt had been bulldozed, and half buried were the old planks from the cabins. I picked up a small board and left.

Up past the infirmary again, then to the volleyball court, now up on our left. As we passed, I stopped and gathered another souvenir—a small rock from the volleyball court wall.

When we got back to the car, we took another look at the turtle. David and I agreed to take it home as a pet and on the spot, named it Ro Li. After that, I put him in his seat, went around to my side, and drove off. We were agreeably silent for a while. David seemed to know that something was going on with Dad, what a marvelous boy he is. As we pulled away, I could not help but sing the old camp song—something I honestly had never recalled since I was in camp, but something that came back to me naturally and with certainty:

> Kai yai, kai yike us, Nobody's like us
> We are the boys of Camp Ro Li.

> Always a grinnin', always a winnin',
> Always a feelin' fine, kai yai!

I sang until I was hoarse.

Part 2

Science Fiction

A Secret

ECRETS. THE ONLY THING better than keeping a secret is telling a secret. I've held this one in for many years now, and I can't stand it any longer. Why all that time? Because this is government secret. That's right, an official United States Navy secret.

I was stationed aboard a ship while in the navy. Every year, we would travel down to the Caribbean and practice war games with other ships. That meant a lot of time steaming around a part of the world known as the Bermuda Triangle.

During my last cruise, we were heading home after three weeks of war game exercises.

Our ship was somewhere southeast of Florida, about two days from our home port. It was nighttime, and most of the crew were asleep. But there were a few of us up, on watch.

On a navy ship at sea, there are many watch stations that must be manned twenty-four hours a day. Besides working a normal eight hours, most sailors also have to stand at least one four-hour watch a day. Most watch standers stay in their work area while on watch. This is true for radio and radar operators, engine room personnel, and bridge personnel. The one major exception to this, however, is the sound and security watch.

The sound and security watch must roam around the entire ship during his four hours on duty much like a cop on a beat. He is charged with ensuring that no fire or flooding hazards exist on the ship and that everything is as it should be. There are specific areas that must be checked once or twice during each watch period, and on the hour, every hour, the sound and security watch must go up to the bridge and report in.

The bridge is located forward and high up on ships and is always manned at sea. The navigator, helmsman, boatswain's mate, and two lookouts are all under the command of the officer of the deck. He in turn is responsible to the captain for all occurrences during the four-hour watch. The officer of the deck is also the person to whom the sound and security watch reports.

On this particular night, I had the sound and security mid-watch and was on duty from midnight to 4:00 a.m. This is a rough watch because four prime hours of sleep are lost, but on this night, I did not mind. It was warm outside, and the sea was calm. There were millions of stars out and not a cloud in sight.

As I made my way up to the bridge for the 2:00 a.m. report, I took the outside route to enjoy the weather. I took my time climbing each set of stairs and stood at the rail for a few minutes, gazing out to sea. There was no moon this night, but the sky full of stars made everything sharp and clear.

I finally reached the bridge level and started to walk forward to the bridge. An older friend of mine, Jackson, was standing starboard lookout tonight, and I looked forward to a quick chat before reporting in. As I approached Jackson, I noticed him staring up at the sky.

"Hey, Jackson, what's up?" I asked.

"What do you think of that?" Jackson replied, pointing up to the right.

"Think of what?" I responded, not seeing anything.

"Look again, Del, right there," he said impatiently, without turning.

I searched the sky, seeing nothing. I was just about to speak when, there I saw it.

It was a red ball in the sky, not much bigger than a dot. It was moving and looked like it would eventually pass in front of the ship, right to left.

"You'd better report this, Jackson," I said, keeping my eyes on the dot.

"Already have, Del, already have," was his distant response.

The door to the bridge suddenly opened, and Mr. Turell, Officer of the Deck, came out.

"Good evening, sir, sound and security reports all conditions normal," I stammered, embarrassed at being caught out on the bridge wing rather than being inside where I belonged.

"Uh huh," he said, as he lifted a pair of binoculars to his face.

As we continued to watch, the dot grew larger as it approached. It was then that I noticed that there were actually three dots flying in a tight formation.

"Jackson, go wake the Captain up," ordered Mr. Turell.

"Aye, aye sir," responded Jackson as he quickly moved off.

I stiffened. The captain is not disturbed unless there is a pretty good reason. I tried a question. "What are they, sir?"

"I don't know," said Mr. Turell. "There are no running lights and no tail exhaust. It isn't like anything I've ever seen."

I also noticed that there was no sound. Since we could not tell how big they really were, we could not guess the distance or altitude, but the objects still looked as if they would eventually pass in front of the ship. They continued to move at a steady speed, still on course.

The bridge wing door opened, and Captain Murray stepped out.

"What have you got here, Mr. Turell?" he asked in a firm tone while looking up at the objects.

"I don't know, Captain. We've had visual on them for about four minutes now and…hey! Look at that!"

The objects had been moving along and were now much larger to our naked eyes. There was still nothing about them to identify them as any type of known aircraft and what happened next confirmed that fact.

They stopped. Oh, they did not decelerate smoothly into a slow stop. They stopped instantly and completely, as one unit. The three objects, still in perfect formation, hovered for about six seconds. Then, with incredible speed, they shot straight up.

We watched, fascinated, and waited for the objects to bank over to level flight again, but they didn't. They continued up, straight up into space until we could no longer see them. They left no trail, no sound. Then they were gone.

"Oh my god!" I said, the first one to speak. Both officers looked at me as if noticing me for the first time. The captain then moved quickly inside, picked up the bridge telephone, and punched the code for the Combat Information Center.

"CIC, Con. What have you got on radar?" he demanded.

A nervous voice responded, "I…I don't know, Captain."

"What do you mean…ah hell!" The captain slammed the phone down and stormed off the bridge heading for CIC.

"The Captain's off the bridge," said the boatswain's mate, an official statement that sounded ridiculous considering all that just had happened.

Captain Murray was gone for about five minutes. Jackson went back out on lookout, and Mr. Turell started scanning the sky from inside the bridge. Feeling like an extra shoe, I walked outside and went up to Jackson.

"What do you think?" I asked in a low voice.

"What do I think?" There was nothing low about Jackson's response. "What do I think? I think we just saw three spaceships from another planet buzz our ship, that's what I think!"

"Oh, come on," I said, trying to be rational. "Weren't they some kind of jet?"

"Well, if they were, it is a type I've never seen before," answered Jackson. "Besides, have you ever seen a jet stop like—"

He stopped talking as Mr. Turell opened the door and said, "Both of you, in here now."

As I entered the bridge, I noticed everyone standing around the captain. When he saw we were within earshot, he started to speak.

"Okay, I know all of you are pretty confused about what we just saw. I just got back from CIC, and they told me the most amazing thing of all."

"Gentlemen, these objects did not track on our radar. Our systems are up and running perfectly, but according to CIC, there was nothing out there at all. They had no idea what I was talking about when I went in there."

The captain's voice was steady, but there was a lot of tension in the air.

"Okay. This is what we are going to do," Captain Murray continued, "all of what happened in the last thirty minutes has just been classified by me, as your commanding officer. You are not to speak of this to each other or anyone else. You will not enter any of this in any log or record book. When we return to port, you are restricted to the ship until such time as Naval Intelligence has a chance to question you about this incident. Until then, not a word. Understood?"

"Yes, sir," came the choral reply.

"Very well then, carry on," said the Captain.

Well, that's it. We pulled into port two days later. Naval Intelligence investigators met the ship at the pier. We all had our turn in the wardroom answering all sorts of questions about what we had seen and the sequence of events. We were also reminded never to speak of the incident ever. Threats of prosecution were hung in the air. And finally, we were dismissed.

Now that I have been out of the Navy for many years, the threats of punishment are meaningless, and I am grateful for that.

The worst part though is that nothing was ever explained to us. I never was informed of any conclusion. Part of me doubts if any was ever reached. And the night sky, well, for me, it will always be a source of mystery.

The Gun

OVER THE YEARS, MY friend, Brian, and I had hiked through many of the wooded areas of northwestern New Jersey. We had walked along the wildest trails and broken through thick brush together on our many trips. In that time, we had acquired many woodsman skills and a general feeling for the great outdoors. We've had our share of adventures too, like the time we surprised a bear cub and its mother, the time we discovered a nest of snakes in a cave we had entered while seeking shelter from a storm, and the time we found a lost little girl and returned her to her parents. But none of our experiences had prepared us for the time when we found the gun.

There had been UFO sightings by the hundreds in an area near the Wanaque Reservoir, but that had been years ago. The land near the reservoir is ideal for hiking and for this reason. Brian and I had decided to explore some of the trails that crisscrossed the mountains there.

The sunlight shined down through the pines and oaks as we set off, each well equipped with backpack and sturdy shoes. The trail was sometimes clearly marked and sometimes barely visible. And we paid close attention to where we were going. At least I thought so. About one hour into the hike, just as we crested a ridge above a small, enclosed valley, I stumbled and fell. Brian, after seeing that I was all right, burst out laughing. I got up, also laughing, and after adjusting my pack, went to see what I had tripped over. Expecting to see a pine root or a piece of rock sticking up, I was more than a little surprised to find a blue/black piece of metal sticking up out of the ground.

"Hey, Brian, look at this," I said, kneeling down for a closer view of the object.

"What is it, Dave?" asked Brian.

"I don't know yet, but I'm going to find out," I answered, taking off my pack.

We each carried a small garden shovel and after taking them out, went to work. We cleared the ground from around the object for a better look and started to dig carefully around it.

The thing appeared to be a rectangular piece of metal stuck solidly in the ground at a slight angle. It seemed to have been buried there for a long time since the ground was uniformly hard around it. As we cleared more of the object, Brian noticed that there was no sign of corrosion on it.

After a few more minutes of digging, we had exposed about a foot of the thing. Besides getting slightly thicker, the object looked the same as before. Then Brian hit a bump with his shovel.

"Dave, move back a bit so I can clear this out better," said Brian.

I moved out of the way, but rather than just stand there, I cleared the surface area out a little further back from the hole, careful not to disturb the object. Brian worked slowly and with caution on this new discovery and soon had it exposed.

Attached to the rectangular object was a small cylinder of metal that ended in a round cone about an inch out. It reminded me of a button and was made of the same material as the rectangle.

After a quick inspection of this new development, Brian and I returned to the digging. It was a few minutes later that we got our next surprise. The rectangular piece was completely dug out, but there was more to the object. It angled off to one side causing us to dig the hole wider as well as deeper. The new section of the thing was flatter than the other piece had been, and as I studied the object more fully, I stopped digging. Something about the shape seemed very familiar to me, and suddenly I had it.

"It's a gun, Brian, it's a gun!" I said excitedly.

"What are you talking about?" Brian replied, getting up and looking down at the object. "How can it be a gun? The handle is way too long, there's no hammer on the thing and...and..." his voice trailed off as his eyes suddenly grew large. We both stared at the thing, thinking incredible thoughts. Finally, I spoke.

"Do you suppose this could have anything to do with all those UFO sightings years ago?"

"Well, it certainly looks like some sort of gun, Dave," Brian said with eerie conviction.

"Yes, it does. I don't know how it can be, but God! There it is, right in front of us!" I was numb.

"Well, let's finish digging it out and see what we've got here," said Brian, fully composed again.

We went back to work.

A few minutes later, the gun laid out on top of the ground. The flat piece stretched out about nine inches from where it joined the handle and then tapered off to a narrow and wicked looking point. Beneath the flat section was a shallow hole that had two tiny recesses at the bottom. As we studied the gun, our guess was that the hole was a sort of magazine slot for whatever the gun fired. One thing was for sure. The weapon was not of this earth. Brian and I decided it was time for a break.

We set the gun down near the edge of the hole and took out our lunches. We sat on the ground and silently ate each to ourselves as we privately came to terms with what we had discovered. Finally, lunch over, garbage packed back in our knapsack, and somewhat rested, Brian and I looked at each other. I spoke first.

"It seems to me that we have two big questions before us. One, if we find a magazine for this gun, should we load it up and test fire the gun? And two, what do we do with the gun. I mean, who gets it?"

"Don't forget question number three," said Brian, looking around. "What else is buried around here?"

"Well," I sighed as I got up, "first things first. Where do you suppose we have to dig to find this magazine thing? Assuming of course, there is one."

"Let's try the easy way first," said Brian. "I'll start right here." He pointed to the hole where we had found the gun.

As Brian started digging at the bottom of the hole, I picked a spot about four feet away and started clearing the leaves. As I started to dig, Brian's question number three popped into my head, and I was suddenly a little nervous about what I might find. Then I heard Brian call, "I've got something."

I looked over just in time to see him pull a bag like object out of the hole. It was made of a woven metal very similar to the type used on the gun and was clearly associated with it. Inside the bag were several objects, and Brian, without a word, reached in and pulled one of them out.

It was a magazine or a power pack of some sort, exactly what we had hoped beyond hope to find. The two prongs on top of the squat cylinder were just right to fit into the magazine slot. Brian and I looked at each other.

"Time to talk," he said.

First, we sat down and took a closer look at the bag and its contents. The bag held not one, but five of the magazines. Each was identical and free from any signs of wear or age, just like the gun. Neither of us felt like putting a magazine into the gun, not just yet anyway.

"We've got to think this through," I said.

"What do you mean?" asked Brian.

"Well, we are going to test fire this thing, aren't we?"

"Sure."

"How do we know how powerful it is? I mean, do we point it at a tree ten feet away and push the button?"

Brian caught on. "The blast from the gun could kill us. We don't even know what this thing shoots. And if ten feet is too close, then what. A hundred feet?"

"I don't know, Brian, but we've got to try. What do you think?"

"I'm in," he said.

We finally decided to hike down into the small valley below us and test fire the weapon there. As we walked down the trail, I noticed a meadow in the valley. It seemed perfect for what we wanted to do. Nearly a hundred yards long and half that wide, the meadow featured a steep wooded slope on one side and a rocky area on the other. Our plan was to fire the gun from behind the shelter of the rocks across the meadow at a tree on the other side. The steep slope beyond the trees would provide a backstop for whatever came out of the gun.

We worked our way over to the rocks and set our packs down. Next, we walked across the meadow and selected a large pine tree as our test target. A red bandana from Brian's first aid kit was tied to the tree to provide the aim point. As we headed back to the rocks, I measured the distance with yard long steps. It turned out to be about eighty-two yards from where we would fire the gun to the target.

Next on our list was to decide who was to actually fire the gun. Since we both wanted to be the first, Brian and I flipped a coin for the honor. I won the toss. Brian then selected a magazine from the bag and gently inserted it into the slot of the gun. It slid in easily, and with a slight click, it locked into place. Brian then turned the weapon over to me. All was ready.

I crouched down behind a large rock and looked across the field. The bandana on the tree was clearly visible, and the mountainous backstop seemed able to handle any blast effect. Brian had backed off about ten feet and was peering at the tree from behind another large rock. The gun felt awkward with its oversized handle, but I settled into a comfortable position. I then noticed that there were no sights along the top of the gun, so I did the best I could to line the gun up with the target.

"Ready?" I said, barely above a whisper.

"Ready," replied Brian.

I pulled the button.

Nothing.

I pulled again. Nothing again. "Dammit! It won't fire."
"Try two hands and pull harder," suggested Brian.

He had a point. If the handle was so long, maybe the hand that was meant to hold the gun was stronger than mine. I regripped the gun in a two-handed grip that placed one index finger on top of the other and prepared to try again.

"Ready?" I checked with Brian again.
"Ready," he responded, still excited. I pulled hard on the button.

I woke up. I was flat on my back in the woods. As I sat up, I felt a tingling throughout my body that nearly forced me back down. Looking around, I saw Brian laid out about ten feet away. He too was just waking up. Slowly, the situation came back to me. I saw the gun lying unchanged on the ground next to my right foot. Looking back to Brian, I said, "Wow! What happened?"
"Talk about backlash," he said. "I wonder how long we were out."
"I don't know, but I'm starting to feel better," I said as I stood up.

I got up facing away from the meadow, looking at Brian. As he got up, I noticed him look past me, and then his eyes went wide. I turned around to look at the meadow.
At first, I couldn't believe what my eyes told me. We had been knocked out by the blast of the gun, but what happened in the meadow, on the receiving end of the weapon, was unbelievable.
The grass in the meadow along the line of fire was gone, burned away. In addition, the soil was pressed down like a great weight had passed over it. At the fringes of where the gun blast had traveled, the

grass was scorched black out to about twenty feet on each side. But that was nothing compared to what we saw when we looked for the target.

The tree was gone, not a sign of it remained. All the smaller trees that had been within fifty feet of the target were also either gone or severely burn damaged. As for the steep backstop, where there had been solid ground a few minutes before, there was now a tunnel, twenty feet in diameter that bored straight into the mountain. At first, we could only see darkness inside from across the meadow, but then it appeared that at the back of the tunnel, there was a reddish glow, as if all the heat from the blast was not quite used up yet.

"Oh my god, Dave, do you believe this?" Brian walked over, taking slow steps. He was still looking at the meadow.

"The power," I stammered. "Imagine what this could do to… to anything!"

"No imagination necessary," replied Brian. "Just look at that," he added, pointing to the carnage in the meadow.

We stood there staring at our handiwork for a few minutes more until finally Brian said, "Okay that takes care of question number one, Dave. What about the issue of who gets it?"

"Yeah, well, let's think about this," I responded, leaning against the rock. "We could turn this over to the FBI or even the military, but somehow that thought scares me."

"I think it would be the same no matter who we gave this thing to," said Brian. "It would end up on a jet or a tank somewhere, killing people."

His faced changed. "I don't think we should give to anyone."

"What?" I wasn't sure what he meant.

"Let's keep it, Dave, just you and me," continued Brian, on a roll now. "Personally, I don't trust anyone I could think of with this amount of power. No one would be able to resist using such a weapon."

"Yeah, well speaking of no one, what about you and me?" I asked.

"We could separate the magazines and the gun. We could make sure they never come together. Then the weapon would be useless, even if one of us got greedy." Brian presented a convincing argument.

"But what about the magazine in the gun right now?" I asked. "And how about the other things that may be buried around here?" There were still a few loose ends.

What it finally came down to was trust. Brian and I trusted each other, and we still do.

The magazine easily slipped out of the gun. We hiked out of the valley and went home and from there, developed our solution. We decided never to discuss what we found or did that day, never to return to that place and to take care of things in our own way.

It's not easy. Once in a while, when we are alone, we do talk about the gun. We speculate about going back with bigger shovels. But we are determined to keep our word to each other.

And we have a little insurance, just in case.

Right now, somewhere near Brian's house, buried in the ground, is a metallic bag with five magazines in it. And in a place near my home, buried deep down, is an alien weapon—a gun. Neither of us knows where both components are hidden, and no one will ever see them again.

Children of the Maya

A ND SO IT WAS not completely unexpected when I first heard reports of the discovery.

After all, December 21, 2012 was a date very much in peoples' minds and general knowledge of the Mayan prediction of the end of the world had been widespread for some time.

Still, that first moment when the news broadcasters announced that something had been detected out in space beyond Saturn and was heading toward the earth, I was shocked.

Thanksgiving was over. The retail frenzy known as Black Friday had recently passed, and we had all settled into that final slow but sure season approaching Christmas. And now this.

The object was first thought to be a new comet, certainly a product of nature, whose course would just so happen to close approach the Earth during the week before Christmas. No big deal.

Then, other details started coming in—announcements that described the object as *slowing down* and *possibly guided by intelligence*. Such revelations drew massive attention, and people of the Earth started to think in new ways. The survivalists bugged out and headed for the hills. Hoarding of food, water, gas, and the like began to strain supply networks throughout the world. We on the northeast coast, who had just been through superstorm Sandy, thought we were better prepared than most, but we too were quickly overwhelmed by the magnitude of the growing panic.

People stopped going to work. Children were kept home from school. At first, not many. Then, reports came in that the object was actually a group of smaller objects, each measuring a mile or two in diameter. In other words, ships of some kind. And they would arrive near enough to enter orbit over Earth on December 21.

That did it. Massive panic swept over millions of people. Urgings by scientists, government officials, military leaders, and clergy were ignored by most. People fled from cities toward the countryside, quickly becoming refugees in makeshift camps on the mountains, fields, and even parking lots. Where was a safe place anyway?

Those of us who decided to stay at home had our own challenges. We increased our efforts to acquire even more supplies, often aggressively. Food, water, tools, and weapons, the list quickly became all encompassing. Windows were boarded up. Doors were barricaded. Some even blocked off the street.

Then the electricity went off. Everywhere. At nearly the same time. No one knew why, but with the rapid approach of the ships, speculation ran high of an impending invasion. The panic level increased to full blown.

Infrastructure started to collapse. Public services, such as police, fire, and garbage collection, ceased. Some communities managed to hold things together but for the most part anarchy ruled. Issues were settled with gunfire.

The most amazing part for me was that all this happened within a month of the initial discovery. As I sit here writing this, I am as prepared for whatever is to come in my own way. Safe? I don't know. How could I? But I am home with my family and the dog. We have food, water, clothing, tools, and weapons.

My generator is full, and I managed to acquire a decent supply of gas. We play cards, read, rehearse first aid and defense techniques, and twice a day, run the radio for news updates. I have coordinated our activities with those of a few of my neighbors. Things seemed to have settled down a bit, at least in our neighborhood.

And so, the Earth waits. Tomorrow is the 21st. We don't know what will happen. But at least the wait will be over.

Rapture

WHEN SIMON WAS A boy of fourteen, he and his dad, Roger, rented a boat and tackle and went fishing while on a vacation in Virginia Beach. Roger motored the boat, while Simon cut the bait up and prepared the poles. The day looked promising, mid-seventies, calm seas, and only the occasional light wind. Once the boat was about three hundred yards offshore, Simon's dad shut down the motor, and the fishing began. It was nearly midsummer, so bluefish were the quarry that day.

As time passed on, Roger and Simon would secure the fishing poles and move the boat to another location in an attempt to find the fish. But as the morning dragged on, it became apparent that this was not going to be a good trip. Roger suggested one more move and then, return to shore. Simon agreed, and Roger started up the boat again.

About fifteen minutes into their last attempt, Simon got a hit. He jerked the pole up and felt the resistance he had set the hook. The fight was on. Since the water was not too deep, the contest didn't last too long. The fish put up a noteworthy struggle but eventually was pulled up near the surface.

"Look at that," Roger said, with an amazement in his voice.

Simon, who had been focused on the mechanics of managing the fishing rod, only looked at his catch after he heard his father's outburst. And then he too was amazed.

He had not caught a fish. When he looked into the water, he saw a mermaid, a young girl with long blond hair and from the waist down, a scaly back end that led to a fishtail. In disbelief, he nearly dropped the pole into the water but quickly recovered.

By this time, the mermaid had leveled out just beneath the surface. Simon could see that the fishhook had caught the left side of her mouth, and she was bleeding from the wound. Her arms were thrashing around, trying to break free of the hook, but Simon could see that she was near exhaustion.

Then their eyes met. She had beautiful blue eyes, though now, full of anguish. She recognized Simon as the predator, and he saw her look change to one of panic and despair. And he had pity on her. As Roger was moving toward him with the net, Simon took out his knife and without hesitation, cut the line. The mermaid, now free, floated in the water for a few seconds and then swam back down to the depths but not before turning and once again, meeting Simon's eyes with a look that said thank you and a brief smile that even with a still bleeding mouth, was beautiful.

"Why did you do that?" Roger asked in a curious voice. He was still a bit shocked at the whole thing.

"I couldn't bring her out of the water, Dad. It would have killed her," replied Simon, still a bit flustered himself.

"What do you mean, her? You talk as if it were a person. It was not. It was a...a," Roger seemed to run out of words.

"A mermaid, Dad, that thing was a real live mermaid," said Simon. "Come on, we both saw it, right?"

"Yeah but...how could that be? Real mermaids do not exist. They are just legends." Simon could see that his father was trying to rationalize.

"I don't know, Dad, but we sure did see it, didn't we?" said Simon.

The trip back to the boat landing was a long one. Roger kept a slow pace which gave them both time to come to terms with what had happened and to devise a plan for *what's next*. They ended up deciding to keep the mermaid encounter a secret and to just tell the rest of the story as it truly was; that is, they did not catch any fish.

At first, it proved exceedingly difficult for Simon not to tell anyone. Part of him wanted to shout out his story to anyone and everyone, but he knew nothing good would come of it. For himself, he pretended it had been nothing more than a dream, a tall tale made up for him one night while he slept. And that helped.

A few years later, Simon went through some dramatic changes. He graduated high school. Tragically, his father was killed in a car accident just a few months later. His mother was left to raise his two younger sisters. Because of these developments, Simon decided to join the United States Navy. He and his mom had discussed his future and concluded that the Navy would provide him with steady work and pay enough so he could send some money home to support the family. Shortly after, Simon enlisted.

Simon did well on his entrance exam and was offered some high-end positions. He selected a career path as a radioman. Simon's choice and his subsequent schooling earned him a higher rank than many of his peers, and it was soon afterward that he was assigned to a destroyer out of Norfolk, Virginia.

Sometime later, while on a four-week underway, Simon was tasked with replacing an antenna module. While moving the new module across the main deck, a sudden and unexpected lurch of the ship caused Simon to lose his balance. He was first thrown against one of the side rails with enough force to open a wound on his right shoulder and nearly dislocate the joint. And then he went over the side and was catapulted into the water.

Others on deck saw Simon get thrown off the ship and soon after, a *Man Overboard* announcement was made over the 1MC, the ship's public address system. As there was no helicopter embarked on this cruise, the small boat crew was assigned as the rescue team. They quickly manned one of the ship's Rigid Hull Inflatable Boats (RHIBs) and were lowered into the water. Even though the ship had immediately reversed its propellers to stop, by the time it actually did stop, it had traveled about a half mile beyond Simon. But overall, things went smoothly, and within twenty minutes, help was on its way.

When Simon hit the water, he was surprised at how cold it was. He did remember his training, and the first thing he did was to remove his heavy boots. Then he started to tread water. But the sea did not cooperate. The wave swells were between three and five feet, and a constant wind kept blowing salty sea spray into his face. Things were more difficult for Simon as he was not wearing a life jacket, and his shoulder injury made his right arm useless for swimming. As a result, it was not long before Simon got tired. His kicking slowed and then stopped, and he began to sink. Shortly after that, Simon felt that he was running out of air. He was underwater, and he was drowning.

And so, a condition known as rapture hypoxia took over his mind. As his brain became more and more starved of oxygen, a sense of calm acceptance swept over Simon. He saw not one but two mermaids' approach. The first one grabbed his arm on his injured side—there was no pain—and started to pull him down. But the other mermaid shooed the first one off, grabbed the same arm, and started pulling him up toward the surface. Not only that, but she also then approached his face and kissed him, giving Simon a fresh breath of air. He then saw that this mermaid was the one, the same one he had let go those many years ago. She still wore the scar from the hook on the left side of her mouth. She was beautiful, and she was saving him.

Simon smiled as he relaxed.

In reality, it was not mermaids that approached Simon. It was a great white shark. It was swimming nearby and detected Simon soon after he had entered the water. After smelling the blood from Simon's shoulder, the shark closed in. The great white bumped Simon on the right arm, a bump that sent him further down. The shark then briefly swam away only to return moments later to bump Simon again, this time propelling him up toward the surface. Sure of its prey now, the shark circled back again, and this time, it bit.

Stepping Out

MY FRIEND JOHN LIVED in a cottage in the hills of western Connecticut. Behind the cottage, there was a small yard and behind that, miles and miles of forest. What made the woods especially nice was the fact that there were many ridges, small valleys, and rugged areas all beneath the thick double canopy.

I would visit John every month or so back in those days, and together we would spend many hours exploring the woods and hills near the cottage. We were always amazed at the abundance of wildlife that lived in or traveled through these woods. As time went on, we developed quite an interest in placing ourselves in adventitious positions so that we could observe the animals of the woods as they went about their business. We called these ventures *stepping out*.

"Hey, John, are you ready for some stepping out this weekend?"

"You bet, Dave," replied John. He sounded excited over the phone.

"We're supposed to get a clear night on Saturday along with a full moon. How is the snow up there?" I asked. The snow tended to last longer in Connecticut than down home in New Jersey.

"We still have about five inches on the ground, and it looks like it will stay cold throughout the weekend," answered John.

"I think this is the weekend we've been waiting for."

He was right. The combination of a moonlit night free of clouds with bright snow on the ground was the ideal condition for stepping out. It would be almost as clear as in daylight. The fact that the temperature would stay well below freezing did not bother us. We had learned long ago how to deal with that.

"It sounds good to me," I said. "I'll see you Saturday afternoon."

"Take it easy, Dave," John said by way of goodbye. We hung up.

Saturday proved to be just as promised, cold and clear. The drive up to John's cottage went quickly and without incident. John had all his gear packed up by the time I got there, and we spent a few hours hanging out, barbequed a couple of steaks, and just talked about old times. Finally, at about six that evening, it was time to go. The moon would be up soon, and we wanted to be in position before it rose.

The snow was dry and powdery, so we made very little noise as we set out. We did our best to tread lightly and after adjusting our packs, felt comfortable with the hike. We whispered a little, but once we got into the woods, we went silent and used only hand signals to communicate. John took point, and we started our evening's adventure, me about ten paces behind.

As we headed up the main trail, one we ourselves had cut a few years back, John set our pace to optimize quietness. We would walk about a hundred steps, then stop for about thirty seconds, and listen. This method, though it slows you down, had always served us well in a way to spot animals before they spotted us. And the fact that there was no wind tonight helped keep our scents close to us, another big advantage.

After about a half hour, we left the main trail and started up along a ridgeline to the spot we would set up for this night. The trail was narrow here and in some places, disappeared altogether, but these were our woods. And we knew them well.

As we continued up the rocky terrain, the moon peeked out atop the adjacent ridge to the east. As it did, everything became much brighter, and we could actually see shadows by the moonlight. John signaled us into a crouch for the remaining few yards to the top of the ridge. We moved extra slowly here because below us was a small valley that was often very busy at night. And sure enough, just before and below us were five deer just meandering out of the valley.

John and I quickly settled in. Each of us removed our pack and took out the ponchos.

This modified raincoat was nothing more than a large square of dark green plastic with a built-in hood. We used it not for protection from rain, but in this case, as a way to disguise our human shape as we perched on top of the ridge.

After the ponchos, we took out our folding chairs. These were of a camper's design and were small, compact, and above all, silent. We didn't want anything squeaking to betray our presence. Next, the binoculars, a compact set with variable magnification. John had the camera tonight, and as I started scanning the depression below us, I could hear him setting up the zoom lens. I had a feeling that tonight would be special, but I wasn't sure why.

Finally, we were ready. John and I took turns observing the valley, he with his camera and me with my binoculars. We moved slowly so to not attract attention and once in a while just remained still. At one point, I spotted an owl on a tree. It seemed to notice something on the ground, probably a mouse. It launched itself from the tree and glided more then flew down to where it snatched something off the ground—a magnificent thing to see. I heard the camera click several times as John tried to capture the event.

Soon after, our next encounter occurred. This was less entertaining and more dangerous. A large dog entered the valley from its northern side. It was a long-haired German shepherd that had been reported by some homeowners as a feral animal, a wild dog that could be a threat to pets and people alike. The authorities had been trying to capture this dog for a while now and had requested anyone spotting it to report the sighting. As John took some photos of the dog, I noted the time. The plan was to call in the sighting as soon as we got back. The dog moved purposely along, its nose to the ground following the path that the earlier deer had taken. It finally wandered off, quietly and on the hunt.

After the dog sighting, John and I were both in need of a stretch. We stood up and stepped back a few yards from the ridgeline and downhill a bit. John took out his portable butane stove, while I got the water out from my pack. I poured the water into our stainless-steel cups, and one by one John heated them up. We then added the coca mix and enjoyed one of the best things about winter activities, a hot drink on a cold night.

"That was the dog I told you about last week," whispered John. "I would not like to meet it face-to-face tonight."

"Yeah, me neither," I whispered back. "Hopefully, when we report our sighting, they will be able to catch it."

John nodded in agreement, and we started to clean up. A few minutes later, we were back on the ridgeline.

The valley looked slightly different, and it took me a few seconds to realize that as the moon had continued to rise, it shed light onto the terrain at a different angle than before. Areas that had been brightly lit were now in shadow and vice versa, and the overall effect was as if we were looking at the valley for the first time. As I scanned with my binoculars, a sudden movement caught my eye. It had appeared, just for an instant, that there was a small boy standing below me in one of the trees, but when I looked again, I saw only branches. Nevertheless, I tapped John's arm twice, and as he turned to me, I pointed to my eyes, then the valley, and then shrugged my shoulders, indicating to him that I thought I saw something but wasn't sure. He took a careful look around and after a while, signaled back that he hadn't seen anything.

Well, that's that, I thought. I was wrong.

A few minutes later, several deer entered the valley from one of the southern pathways. All were doe except for the last one which was a six-point buck. I counted six of the deer. They walked slowly and cautiously as deer always do. They seemed to follow nearly in each other's footsteps, and I could hear John taking picture after picture of them. I hoped the money we had spent for the custom work to muffle the sound of the shutter click would pay off, and indeed, it seemed to be working. Though I could hear the sound each time John took a picture, it was apparent that the deer didn't.

The deer by this time had spread out a little bit and started to browse for food. John and I relaxed a little and just enjoyed watching them. All was peaceful.

Then the lead deer looked up and stiffened. Her tail twitched side to side as she flexed her ears in all directions. She had alerted to something and was searching. Had she detected us? John and I got as still as we could as the waiting game commenced. All players remained frozen for a couple of minutes before finally, the doe relaxed and went back to her grazing. I breathed a silent sigh of relief.

Just then to my surprise, from the very tree, I thought I had seen something in, an object leaped down and landed right on the back of the lead deer. It looked, it looked just like a little boy covered with long black hair. The creature wrapped itself tightly around the deer's neck and seemed to start biting the deer as it leaped around in an effort to get free. I caught a terrible glimpse of a blood-soaked face as the creature pulled up from the deer only to dive in again to bite its neck. The other deer scrambled madly away, and John and I both stood up, not believing what we were seeing.

Finally, the deer fell. It twitched a few times on the ground but was clearly finished. The creature hung on tightly for a, while after the deer stopped moving until finally it too had finished. As it slowly unraveled itself from the dead deer, John and I gave each other a quick glance and unsheathed our knives. Though they were seven-inch Ka-Bar knives, I remember thinking that they may not be big enough.

The creature stood up. Looking again, I saw that it could not be human. It had very short legs and overly long arms, all covered with thick hair. Its face, however, was hairless, although now covered with blood. It stood slightly away from its kill and briefly looked it over. Then it squatted down a bit and looked up at the moon. Its head flew back as it opened its mouth and started to howl at the moon. The sound was high-pitched and very frightening, but John and I were too far gone to care. As one, we also began to yell and howl with knives raised, not at the moon but at this horrible little thing that had savaged our souls.

The creature froze in mid-howl and turned to look at us. Its gaze held us steady for several seconds as if measuring us and the threat we represented. Then it yelped once, perhaps in fear, perhaps in disappointment, and faster than thought, ran away and out of the valley. Its gait reminded me of a gorilla.

John and I stopped yelling. After a long few moments, we put our knives away and took in the situation. The deer lay down there, still before us as a reminder that this had actually happened. But we did not look at it. We both stared for many minutes at the spot where the creature had disappeared, daring it to come back and praying it would not.

The trip back to the cottage that night was exhausting. Not so much for the physical side of things but for the fact that we were hyperalert. We had been woodsman for a long time and knew the value of staying calm. We had packed all our gear back up and started down the ridgeline for the main path. But once there, the paranoia kicked in. Both of us felt it. We pulled our knives back out as we expected to be ambushed at any moment. The moonlight illumi-nated our way back but could also expose us to danger, a level of danger we had never faced before. At one point, we looked at each other and actually laughed, a pathetic attempt to get back to normal, but it helped.

Finally, back at the cottage, we were able to talk about our expe-rience. We went over every minute of the evening and decided to keep everything about the creature to ourselves. It just wouldn't make sense to tell anyone about it. We ended up calling the police about the dog but didn't mention anything else. Let them figure it was the dog that killed the deer. We didn't care.

These days of course, John and I remain friends and continue to get together on occasion.

But things are different now. He lives in New York City. And for both of us, the stepping out gear is somewhere buried in our closets.

Daydreaming

E VER SINCE I WAS a boy, I have always been a window watcher, one of those people peering out the window of a plane. I was always fascinated by what was *down there* and how it looked from *up here*. Whenever I flew, I would always ask, beg, or demand a window seat and spend much of the trip gazing out into the void. My nose would be pressed against the plastic window, neck kinked to the right or left, and my body awkwardly twisted forward and to the side to look down either in front of or behind the jet's wing.

But it was always worth it. I remember on a recent trip to San Diego, as we passed over the Rockies and southern Nevada, I was taken aback by the beauty of the terrain. The sand with hues of red and yellow, the sheer cliffs, and the random ridgelines of the hills and mountains all stood out. The streams and rivers snaked through it all like frozen serpents in the sand.

Occasionally, I'd see a roadway or a bridge or the reflection off a series of buildings, but from six miles up, it all looked still and lifeless.

It's funny how time can stretch. How a mere moment of real time can contain hundreds of micro-images, feelings, thoughts, and memories. How, as time marches on at its normal pace, you can get lost in powerful flashbacks of minutes, days, or even weeks of experience. And always, the jolt back to reality brings with it a sense of loss and disappointment.

But there is no time for that now. Yes, the terrain below reminds me strongly of southern Nevada. There below me now is the desert, the sand, the mountains, and the cliffs—that same impression of stillness. But there are no roads, no houses and only ancient dry riverbeds. Because this is Mars, and I am on final approach to our first manned landing site. No time for daydreaming.

Last Day Down the Shore

ONE DAY DOWN THE shore, I was lying on my blanket. The sun was out. The air was warm, and the sea breeze was delightful. I had spent most of the morning between swimming in the ocean and sunbathing on the blanket, and now I was thinking about lunch.

But it was comfortable, and I did not want to get up. So I laid my head back and closed my eyes.

Then I heard a soft thump next to me that brought me back awake. I blinked my eyes a few times and turned to see what had caused the sound. To my surprise, a sandwich lay on the blanket next to my right shoulder. It was wrapped in a thin clear-looking package and the roll bulged with the promise of ham, cheese, tomato, and lettuce. I did not realize how hungry I was until I saw it.

I quickly sat up and looked around. Had someone walked by and dropped their sandwich? A quick scan showed that though there were others on the beach, no one was close enough to have dropped the sandwich. And so, I took a chance.

Unwrapping the sandwich was easy, and without much fanfare, I took a bite, a big one. Expecting to taste the flavors of a cold-cut sandwich, I was surprised to instead taste something like soggy seafood. And at the same moment, I felt a sharp pain in my lower right jaw, just behind my teeth.

With all this happening, I also noticed something extending from my mouth. There was a thin nearly transparent string hanging down to the sand, and from there, the string seemed to lead into the sea. As I noticed all this, the string suddenly went taut, and the pain in my mouth increased dramatically as I was pulled forward face first into the sand. The strength of the pull increased at that point, and I realized I was being pulled into the ocean.

My initial reaction was one of panic, but I was able to maintain some control. My right hand started flailing up, trying to grab hold of the string as I brought my left hand down to my swimsuit pocket where I kept a small folding knife. At that point, I had been dragged very close to the waters' edge, and the pain was so intense that part of me just wanted to give up. But with a last-ditch effort, I opened the knife and slashed at the string. It separated as the knife cut through. I slid to a stop and watched the string disappear into the water.

I laid there for a while in both misery and relief, just catching my breath. As my thought processes returned, I sat up and looked around. *What the hell just happened to me?* I thought.

I got up rather clumsily and made my way back to the blanket. My mouth was numb with pain. As I stood there, I realized I still had something in my mouth with a string attached. I reached up and pulled the thing out of my mouth. Immediately, I was met with a small torrent of blood, so I grabbed my T-shirt, spun the end into a tight knot, and pressed it onto the wound. I then clamped my teeth together to hold it in place. It looked silly as hell, but I knew it would stop the bleeding.

I then looked at what had been in my mouth. It looked like some sort of hook but was not made of metal. Instead, it looked to be made of bone or rock. Coral? And the string, it resembled plastic but was something else, more organic-looking. And it was not tied to the hook but rather embedded in it.

By this time, I had settled down to a rather normal state of calmness. And so, I began looking for reasons. *What exactly is going on here?* came to mind.

I looked around again seeking a logical explanation. Had I been caught by an errant fishing hook from a trawler or other fishing boat? A quick scan showed nothing of the kind offshore from where I stood. What about a fishing hook and line that was just washed up with the waves? That made sense until I thought of the sandwich.

I then took another look at the sandwich that still lay on the sand where I had dropped it. It had been laying in the sun for about ten minutes by now, and already, much had changed about it. It now resembled more of an oval-shaped blob then a sandwich. All its features had softened as if it was rapidly decomposing. And seeing that changed everything for me.

I realized at that point that what happened here could not be explained logically. What happened here was right out of a *Twilight Zone* episode. Real to me but bizarre to anyone else. I knew what had happened. Something had tried to capture me, drown me, and possibly eat me.

Something that lived in the sea. And something intelligent enough to utilize tools and bait. And lastly, something probably not human.

And so, as I left the beach for the last time, dragging my blanket like a two-year-old, I knew I could never tell anyone about this. Though the string and hook remained on the sand, it was nowhere near enough evidence to convince anyone of, well, anything.

But I also knew I could never hold such an experience inside. Nor could I pretend that this had never happened. And if I tried, I was sure that over time, it would drive me crazy. I had to think of an outlet, some way to let at least part of it go. Perhaps if I wrote it down.

Big Bear

BIG BEAR WAS THE largest of the clan, and as such, he was their leader. His name reflected the respect all had for him as he was named after the land's most dangerous occupant. Big Bear's word was the final one in any dispute, but he was a fair ruler. He would consider all sides of a conflict before rendering a decision. Most of the times such things happened at clan gatherings, and one such event was scheduled for this very night.

The gathering of the clan would be held in the most sacred of all the ancient assembly points, where the ends of two major mountain chains met up with the high meadow of the moon. The thick woods surrounding the meadow as well as the large expanse of grass ensured a comfortable yet spacious area for the meeting. All branches of the clan had been summoned for many issues needed to be resolved.

As was customary, Big Bear was the last to arrive. Most of the clan groups had been at the site throughout the day, and there had been much mixing among them. The mood was generally good, but as Big Bear approached, all returned to their groupings to await their leader.

In the late afternoon sun, Big Bear could feel as well as see his clan assembled along the terrain of the high meadow. The Deep Woods group seemed heavily represented as word of their many issues had already reached Big Bear's ears. He recognized many elders from the Falling Water group as well as those from the Cave Dwellers. The ones that had been his chief allies through all conflicts were gathered nearest, those of the Long Grass group.

After taking this all in, Big Bear jumped up upon the Gathering Rock. He then addressed the crowd.

"Greetings to you all," he spoke. His voice had a deep yet comforting tone that had the effect of both quieting and calming those before him.

"We gather this evening once again in peace and prosperity, thanks to you all, and to resolve any issues that have come between us. But, of course, first things first. I stand before you now as leader and therefore, open myself up to any challenger who wishes to take my place. If you desire to challenge, please step forth at this time."

As he spoke these words, Big Bear pushed out to show his enormous size, and his eyes seemed to catch fire as he scanned the crowd. There was some stirring among the older youths of the Deep Water group, but in the end, no one stepped up. Big Bear allowed some time to pass and then moved on to other business.

"Now is the time for each group to send forth its petitioners. I will accept any and all petitions and make judgments upon them at this time."

This was by far the most important part of the clan meeting. Each group sent a representative to Gathering Rock to voice the group's situation, requests, observations, and even suggestions to their leader. Announcements of pairings, births, and deaths were also made. It was a very necessary ritual that served to keep the clan as a whole together and under one ruler, a tradition spanning time immortal.

And yet, for Big Bear, this tradition, especially his role as leader, was becoming tiresome. He had been clan leader for many years, and though his obligated requests for challengers were delivered with ferociousness, part of him wished for a challenger to accept and even take over, even though it would mean his death. His role in the clan, once executed with joy and enthusiasm, was becoming tedious.

But, in spite of this, Big Bear continued on with his duty. One by one, as each petitioner came forward, Big Bear gave them his undivided attention, listened carefully, and then spoke, sometimes after long meditation. His answer after all was to become the law, so he had to be careful to show both wisdom and justice.

At one point where the conflict of territorial infractions remained heated between the Deep Woods group and those of the Big Trees group even after Big Bear's council, he allowed the final resolution to be rendered in the ancient way—mortal combat. Each group sent out its best warrior, and there, in the clearing next to Gathering Rock and before the entire clan, the combat took place.

The issue was resolved in the Deep Woods group's favor, and all joined together to mourn the loss of a great warrior and to congratulate the victor. When the excitement drew down, Big Bear once again addressed the crowd.

"There is one more issue that we must consider before this gathering comes to a close. The moon is rising, so I will not speak at length.

I am concerned about the human encroachment into our territories. Word has reached me that humans are appearing all along the eastern limits of our lands. They are killing our trees and changing the natural appearance of the land. They are constructing large, wide paths through woods and fields. They are building structures that look like little hills with holes in them, and they live inside these things. They are venturing into our woods, mountains, and valleys. And worst of all, they bring fire, something that is forbidden to us.

If we kill them, it would only invite more, and then they would come rapidly and in great numbers. And so, I have decided what we will do. We are going to avoid them and remain hidden from them. It should be easy as they are a slow and clumsy people. But they will not go away. We will have to share our territories with them. They are but a few now, and though I believe others will come, it should be at a slow pace.

So, I say to you now, remain hidden from these humans. Do not let them see you, hear you, or encounter you in any way. We must bury our dead deep so they will never be discovered. And if we are seen, we must run away, never fight. All conflicts between our groups shall be secondary to the decree of avoiding the humans. Does everyone understand?"

Big Bear scanned the crowd as all nodded their heads. He sensed much anxiety in many of those before him, so he concluded, "But do not fear. Our way of life will continue with or without these humans. The world is vast, and it extends even beyond our lands. So return to your realms, and as the full moon rises, be at peace."

And with that, Big Bear gave his leaders' howl as the bright full moon appeared over the nearby meadow. The clan, as a single voice, howled in response, the sound booming over meadow and hill alike. And so, the gathering ended.

As the clan dispersed, Big Bear remained atop Gathering Rock, his image a reassurance to any who looked back. He stood tall and watched as his people departed. Though he didn't show it, his concern for this human situation played heavily on his mind. He knew change was coming. And it would make life for the clan more difficult.

Finally, he was once again alone. Big Bear jumped down and started his long journey home. His bodyguards appeared out of nowhere and followed him as he considered the future of his race. As he walked back to his home territory, Big Bear of the Meadow Rock group of the Sasquatch Clan took a long cautious look around as he crossed the high meadow before a full moon.

The Crossing

I T WAS A BRIDGE crossing that looked like it had existed over hundreds of years. The actual bridge looked modern enough, concrete over steel girders and metal fencing along the edges, but it was the place that drew my attention.

I am just a wanderer now. I tried normal living. I got a degree in chemistry, a job at a pharmaceutical company, a large home in the suburbs, a gas guzzling Camaro, a purebred Vizsla, and a wife who loved money and me, in that order. When the money was gone, she left and gave me a chance to reevaluate my life. You know the routine. But my decision was to hit the road, literally. I'm walking now. Have feet, will travel.

And I have seen some things too—fires in the meadowlands, miles wide. Tornado tracks ripping through woods, houses, and mini malls like a knife through butter. But this bridge crossing piqued my interest as soon as it came into view.

The crossing itself was not too dramatic. Overall, about a twenty-five-foot drop off in the terrain with a slow meandering stream at the bottom. This part of rural Pennsylvania had hundreds of such crossings.

But what caught my eye was the well-worn path that took you off the road and down under the bridge. *A great fishing spot* was my first thought, but it seemed there was something more. And it drew me.

Before I knew it, my feet had me on the path and off the road. Well-worn indeed, the path angled down sharply at first but soon tapered off to a more moderate decline. The brush, although thick, appeared trimmed back somewhat to make the pathway more inviting. And the transition from the hot, sunny dead air on the road to the cool shadowy stream breeze was refreshing. As I reached the end of the path, I could see more detail of the steam itself.

It was a small stream, a brook really, about twenty to thirty feet across as it moved along at a steady but not rapid pace. Its bottom was strewn with a mix of pebbles and soft sandy soil. A path, very similar to mine, coursed up alongside the bridge on the far side. It seemed odd that the two pathways were the only cleared areas by the stream that no one had bothered to open up a space along the streambed on either side.

Then I saw the old man. He was close, and I was a bit startled at first for in my concentration on the stream, I hadn't noticed him standing right next to me. He was dressed in a black outfit of shoes, pants, and shirt, and his weathered face was half hidden beneath the brim of a large hat, also black. In his right hand, he held a staff of near black ancient wood.

"Care to cross?" he asked. "Only fifty cents. A quarter for each eye," he added with what sounded like a chuckle.

"How would I do that?" I asked, nervous but not yet sure why. "I don't see a boat or a raft."

"No need, my friend. Just climb on my back, and I will carry you to the other side." His voice sounded like cloth sliding across a tabletop.

"That makes no sense," I replied. "I could just go back up the way I came and cross the bridge."

"That is certainly true," said the old man, "but such a crossing would give you nothing you do not already have. Come with me, and I offer you a new life."

My neck hairs stood up.

"Who are you?" I asked in a cautious tone.

"You know who I am," he replied. "Every man is a shining star unto himself until dimmed by the dark companion."

"That's not funny," I said.

"I am never funny. Come," he beckoned.
I ran.
Up the path. Out into the sunlight. Up onto the road. The road. Oh no! The truck!

Waiting

WHEN I WAS A boy, my grandparents lived out in the country by Milford, New Jersey.

Their yard was woods and open meadow. On occasion, my parents would leave me with gramps and grams for the day or the weekend.

I was always made to feel welcome, and my days were filled with activities. My grandparents would take me to town or to restaurants along the Delaware River. My grandma would let me help cook, and Grandpa would take me for hikes in the woods. Among my favorite activities, however, were my solo trips to the meadow behind the house. It was huge and covered an expansive hill. I would spend hours exploring this meadow, careful always to stay within earshot in case Grandpa called me back to the house.

On an early summer day during my tenth year, a day like many others, warm, bright, and clear, I stood in the meadow with grass up to my hips. Wildflowers and bees were all around, and an occasional hawk would fly over me on its own mission of exploration. I was comfortable in my surroundings so when I noticed a silver ball high up in the sky I was not alarmed, merely curious. At first, I thought it was a balloon, but as it got closer and larger, I recognized that it was being flown and not just riding the winds.

The ball continued to descend and got bigger. It was perfectly round and silvery in color, though its lower hemisphere seemed to reflect an impression of the meadow, my meadow, below. I felt a twitch of excitement as I realized this thing, whatever it was, was coming my way. I crouched in the tall grass and waited and watched.

The descent continued until the ball made contact with the ground about fifty yards away and uphill from where I was hidden. It rested without sound or movement for a few minutes. I was just about to stand up and walk toward the object, now a spaceship in my mind, when something odd happened.

A round hole appeared in the lower half of the object. It was black and seemed to be an opening into the craft's interior. After a few seconds, something appeared at the doorway and gently floated to the ground, a drop of about eight feet. The object looked like a miniature version of the ship itself, but when it contacted the ground, it changed its shape.

It now looked like a two-level silvery snowman with three legs standing it up and three tentacle-like arms extending from its top section. Then I noticed a third ball, somewhat compressed, on top. I realized that I was looking at some sort of living thing—something from another world.

I was shocked, but my curiosity kept me from running away. I wanted to see if the creature would be joined by a companion, but nothing else came out of the ship.

After a minute or two, the alien started to move around. Its three legs gave it a whipping around motion each time it took a step, and I almost laughed at how ridiculous it looked. The arms each moved independently, and as the creature moved about, they stretched out and began taking up pieces of the grass and other plants of the meadow. The creature had no facial features that I could see but seemed to know enough to select certain samples.

After a few more minutes of observation, I decided to make my move. I remained crouched, but I started to sneak up on the alien to see how close I could get. It was a game I had played many times with deer and birds, and I had become quite stealthy. The creature continued to explore and collect samples as I moved in until finally, I had managed to close the distance between us to a scant fifteen yards.

It was at this time that I started to get what can only be described as *impressions*. The creature made no sounds, yet I seemed to pick up its thoughts. *Strangeness, open,* and *much activity* floated into my head from an outside source that could only have been the alien. I felt no hostility, so I made my second move, probably the bravest thing I have ever done in my life. I stood up.

As I revealed myself to the creature, I received a torrent of impressions. *Alarm. Fear. Escape* bombarded me as I stood there. The impressions were intense but not painful. Though I still could not see any sensory organs on the creature, there was no doubt it was aware of my presence. It whip-ran toward its ship with amazing speed but stopped just short of going in. It paused, and as it did so, I received other impressions: *Curiosity, other*, and *not same*.

I then realized that this alien was one just like me, an explorer, not of meadows but of worlds. And I was amazed. I didn't want to scare it off, so I tried thinking at it in the hope of starting a two-way communication. I thought, *Friend, explorer*, and even *welcome*.

The result was immediate and a bit frightening. The alien whip-stepped toward me so quickly that I had no time to move. It stood before me not five feet away. It was slightly taller than I was, and I now could see features that I had earlier missed. There were two small pocket-like openings in the lower section from which the grass samples stuck out. And along the center of the small uppermost section was a row of small bumps. Eyes perhaps? And finally, at the end of each of its arms were three smaller tentacles just like fingers on my own hands.

We stood there unmoving for a few seconds when I spoke out loud and said, "Hello." The creature reacted by stepping away from me as if the sound had shocked it. But since I remained motionless and silent, it eventually stepped back closer, and I got another impression. This one was more like a question. *Dominant life?*

I thought back, *Yes.* I tried a question, *Others on ship?*

No was the answer. *Alone.*

It seemed almost sad.

It was at this time that my grandfather decided to call me home for supper. As his voice boomed up the hill and over the meadow, the creature took alarm. The impression was intense fear, almost panic; and faster than thought, the alien whip-stepped back to the ship. There was no last-minute pause this time. The creature leaped up through the hole, the opening closed up, and within seconds, the ship itself lifted off, quickly, smoothly, and without a sound.

I was shocked at how fast things went bad and had barely enough time to think *come back* at my new friend. But as the silvery orb grew smaller and smaller in the sky, I did receive one last impression, *Return soon*. And then it was over.

Years passed. As they did, I reflected on my torments. They are many. My grandparents, as loving and open-minded as they were, tried to convince me that I had merely fallen asleep in the meadow and dreamed the entire encounter. They told my parents the *cute* story I had made up. I saw the writing on the wall. I was not a stupid boy. I ended up admitting to Dad and Mom that even though it seemed real, it was probably all a dream.

But as I grew older, what had happened to me became more and more real. I looked forward to visiting my gramps and grams only to return to the meadow and gaze up at the sky. I carried a sketch book and drew from memory countless images of what I had seen, determined not to let it fade away.

Oh, I did tell my story to others, trusted friends and the occasional girlfriend, only to suffer the same reactions—laughter, dismissal, even polite understanding, all based upon disbelief. And so, I learned to shut up about it, to hold it all inside.

When my grandparents' house passed to new owners, I would visit them and ask permission to walk up to the meadow for old time's sake. The owners, John and Mary Baldwin, were good about it, and I would send them cards and gifts to keep the relationship fresh. I would bring girlfriends out there for what they thought were romantic walks. Later, when I got married and fathered two wonderful children, we'd all go to the meadow for picnics and camping trips. And all the while, my gaze would stray up, up to the blue sky of daylight and the starry expanse of the night.

But my alien friend never returned. The sky to me remained empty.

Finally, there came a time when the property was sold to a large corporation, and I was denied access. A solar farm now sits atop my precious meadow. I was heartbroken but soon rationalized a new hope.

Maybe the alien and I have a bond that somehow transcends the meadow, the location where we met. Maybe our bond is psychological in that when (he) does return, we will be able to find each other no matter where we are. Oh, I know that sounds outlandish, even for me, but hey, why not? *Return soon* was the message, was it not? I always thought that it meant return to me personally, not return to the meadow, the earth, the galaxy. And of course, *soon* meant, well, soon—today, tomorrow, next week. But now that I sit here, at fifty-five years old, I'm beginning to think that *soon* may be an interval of time beyond my life span. But no, it could be tonight. And so, I will do what I have been doing for nearly half a century now. I'll wait and wait and wait.

Special

I AM A TECHNICAL WRITER. I write for companies about the products they produce. When you purchase a lawn mower or a microwave oven or nearly anything else, you get some sort of instruction manual. Well, that's me. I write instruction manuals. As I like things precise and logical, technical writing for me is a good fit. I admit to little curiosity and almost no imagination, and I usually don't mix well with others. But that's okay. I don't mind the isolated life. My job is one I can do remotely from anywhere, so I work from home.

I used to live in northwestern New Jersey where the mountains dominate the terrain.

Though I was not far from town, my actual house was set at the end of a long winding driveway. I was literally in the woods—nice and quiet.

My office was located in one of the upstairs bedrooms, and I had a pretty comfortable setup. As far as entertainment is concerned, I usually did not watch much television. Most of my spare time was spent either on my hobby which is building model ships or taking walks in the woods. It was on such a walk one day that I found what was soon to be a companion of sorts.

It started when I was walking on a newly discovered trail. I smelled something odd. The odor seemed out of place and was actually quite pleasant. I stopped and looked around.

There, almost at my feet, was what appeared to be a puppy dog. The odor seemed to be coming from it. There was no den or hole in the ground to suggest a home. I looked around for signs of its mother but after several minutes, concluded that this puppy was alone, either lost or abandoned. So I picked it up and brought it to the house.

Once home, as I took a closer look at my new pet, I noticed a few things out of the ordinary for a dog. Though it had a puppy's face, its eyes seemed large and were a light blue green in color. The ears were normally placed but seemed layered as if they could be extended. The hair was short and dense but among the follicles were thicker hairs that seemed to have tiny holes in them. Four legs and a short tail completed the animal. Most odd, there were no signs of a reproductive organ or even an anus—extraordinary. And so, I decided on the spot to name (him) *Special*.

Over the next few weeks, I learned many things about Special that were very strange. For example, he never barked. Instead, on occasion, I would hear and even feel a low frequency hum from my *dog*. The humming would usually be accompanied by Special looking at me as if he was expecting something. During such a time, the humming would vary in pitch and interval but after a while, would stop.

Another thing that seemed odd were the odors. Special was constantly exuding a smell of some kind. Most often the odors were not unpleasant, definitely an animal-type smell not uncommon to most dogs. But at other times, the odors would be different, like wildflowers or marshlands or even a hint of nuts and berries. These were certainly not dog-like.

One such odor appeared when, as I eventually figured out, Special wanted to go outside.

And when we did go out, another strange behavior became evident.

I had tried to feed Special on several occasions. I tried scrapings from my dinner plate, different types of meat, and just about every kind of dog food I could get my hands on, all to no avail. He had never appeared hungry or thirsty for that matter. But whenever we went out, I noticed that Special went on the hunt.

Special's idea of hunting was not normal for a dog. He did not prowl but instead found a sheltered spot and stood very still. At this time, he displayed another behavior I found astonishing. Special seemed to change both his shape and his coloration to mimic the surroundings. Even to my eyes, he would appear to be a rock or a clump of leaves and branches. At this point, Special would release an odor that I could only think of as a lure, a bait smell that attracted both insects and mice to him. Special would remain motionless as these creatures approached him, getting so close as to nearly touch his face.

When that happened, Special would capture his prey more like a chameleon than a dog. His mouth would open, and a long tongue would shoot out so quickly that it was hard to see. But after a few observations, I was able to discern exactly what happened.

Like a chameleon, Special had a longer tongue than any normal dog. But unlike a chameleon, Special's tongue featured not a sticky blob at the end but a series of small tentacles, like fingers on a hand. These then grabbed the prey whether insect or rodent and held it firm while the tongue retracted. There was no chewing. The prey seemed to be swallowed whole.

This would repeat until Special was full. At that time, he would first change his appearance back to his normal shape and color and then emit an odor that was pleasant for me. I assumed it to be a signal he was done, and so I brought him back inside.

Now, with all this odd behavior, one would think that I would call a veterinarian or someone similar to report all this. But these events took place after a period of time—a time when I was getting used to a companion I didn't even realize I both needed and wanted. Special was indeed *special* to me. He would give me pleasant odors. Whenever I carried him or petted him, he would reward me with a look and emit a low hum that reminded me of a cat's purring.

As described, I lived an isolated life with a profession that was *dry* by most standards. I had no family to speak of, no girlfriend, and very few acquaintances of any kind. So when Special entered my life, I found something that I welcomed and liked. And of course, that made me somewhat blind to certain realities.

Over the next few months, things continued much the same. I would work up in my office, while Special remained downstairs. One element he shared with most dogs was that he spent a lot of time resting, curled up on either the floor or on a bed of towels and blankets I had made for him. When I had finished work, I would take Special either down to my workshop where I would spend some time on the ship models, or we would go for hikes in the woods. Most times, I ended up carrying Special as his short legs made for slow walking. Afterward, he would rest in the living room, while I ate supper. Special would signal me every few days, and I would take him out into the woods near the house and sit while he hunted for his food. It usually didn't take too long.

It was during this time that I developed a few theories about Special. I figured that his emissions of odors served several purposes. One such purpose was communication. I was able to recognize his desire to go out for hunting and to return afterward by the type of smell he emitted at the time. He also used an odor to attract his prey. And finally, I concluded that by emitting odors, somehow Special was ridding his body of waste products. The thickened hairs on his body seemed to support that idea.

As for the humming, I assumed that too was used to communicate satisfaction. That it may have actually been a sophisticated language did not enter my mind until later, when it was almost too late.

Even with these insights of imagination, rare indeed for me, I continued my routine with Special and began to think of it all as normal. As the weather warmed, I started to leave my door open to allow Special to venture out as he wanted to hunt or just lay in the sun. Things moved along at a slow and steady pace.

Then came a day that changed my life. Special had shown me some odd behaviors in the past, but his final reveals were both the most bizarre and the most tragic.

After a particularly long session at work, I came downstairs for my usual time with Special before supper. When I looked for him on the living room floor, he was not there. I was going to head outside when I spotted Special. He was on the wall of the living room. I realized in a flash that Special must have an ability to climb walls, perhaps with suction cups of some kind on his paws. He had never demonstrated this ability before, and I was soon to find out why.

As I looked at Special, I noticed other things as well. His blue-green eyes seemed even larger than normal and were fixed on mine. He was humming at me in a way that did not indicate pleasure or satisfaction. And his color was shifting.

Suddenly things escalated. The humming increased and became very complex, almost like a language. Special's eyes, still staring into mine, started to alternate from their familiar blue green to bright red. It seemed like a warning.

As I went to grab Special off the wall, I heard what I immediately recognized as a mountain lion growl behind me. Somehow the cat must have just wandered in through the open door, and as I turned, it appeared in front of me only seven feet away. Its ears were back, and its eyes were fixed on my face. I knew it was about to charge.

Unbeknown to me, Special had been on the move. His suctioned feet had allowed him to climb not only the wall but the ceiling as well. He had walked the ceiling until he was just above the cougar. The first I became aware of all this was when Special, all twelve pounds of him, leaped from the ceiling and landed right on the head of the cat. I had seen Special hunt many times by then but had never seen him fight. He was amazing. As fast as I could follow, Special changed his coloration over and over again. His humming noises became the loudest I had ever heard and bordered on painful to my ears. And his smell, he put out an odor so powerful that it assailed my sense of smell and nearly drew tears to my eyes.

This sudden onslaught of sight, sound, and smell clearly affected the cougar as it arched its back and shook violently side to side, throwing Special onto the floor. As disoriented as the cat was, however, and true to its character, it pounced as soon as it saw Special in front of it.

Special had not let up on his attack during this time, but it was not enough. The cougar pinned Special to the floor with one paw, leaned forward, and gave him a fatal bite.

Though all of this only took a few seconds, Special's attack on the cat allowed me enough time to retrieve my pistol from the lamp table drawer. I took aim and fired just as the cougar had finished with Special and was once again turning to me. The cat fell dead to the floor, and everything grew very quiet.

It took a few minutes to calm down, and I felt a sense of relief that I was still alive. But it was short-lived. Special, my Special, was dead. There was no doubt. Whatever he had been, he was no more. His body laid still on the floor, blue green eyes now faded to gray, the foul stench of his fight-mode now fading in the air—dead and gone.

In the aftermath, after burying Special and cleaning up all evidence of him, after reporting to the police about the death of the cougar, after cleaning up the house, and bringing everything back to normal, only then did I really sit down with myself and think about Special.

Special was not a dog. I knew that soon after I brought him home the first time. But because he resembled a dog, I ended up treating him like one—my pet dog. I accepted Special into my life even though he displayed behaviors that could not be explained or compared to anything I knew. I was never concerned for my safety. Neither was I inclined to notify anyone, such as a veterinarian or scientist, even though I knew such a person would be able to shed a light on my situation.

Deep down, I knew Special had abilities that demanded more scrutiny. The odors, the humming, and his ability to climb walls and ceilings, all these things suggested at least an entirely new species of an earthbound animal and at the other end of the spectrum, perhaps even an alien life form. But at the time I was too lonely, infatuated, and ignorant to want to do anything about it.

What I did realize soon after Special's death was that I no longer wished to be alone that isolation was not the lifestyle I wanted to pursue any more. That is why I recently sold my house in the woods of New Jersey and moved out here to San Francisco. I want to experience the hustle and bustle of city life. My profession as a technical writer never did take a hit. I am just as capable of meeting my deadlines here as I was in my rural home, so work is not an issue. But I am looking forward now to working in an office. It will give me a chance to meet and mingle.

With people, that is. Time for a change.

Guardian Angel

I HAVE A GUARDIAN ANGEL. Finally, after nearly a lifetime of occasions, now, I am sure. He told me so only yesterday. It confirmed what I had suspected for a long time but of course, had no proof.

It all started when I was just a boy. There may have been incidents prior to this one, but this is the earliest I remember.

One morning during my second-grade school year, I arrived late for school. In those days, children in my area walked to school, even on rainy days, such as the one that morning. I had overslept and from there, all went downhill. Getting yelled at by your mom was not a good way to start a day.

When I arrived at school, the bell had already rung, and most of the children were in the classrooms. I remember as I walked down the hallway and was approaching my class, I saw a little boy and his mother walking the other way. As they passed me, the boy looked me right in the eyes and said, "Don't worry, it will be all right." It was a strange thing to say, and I watched as they continued down the hall, but the boy never turned around.

As soon as I entered the classroom, I went to hang my raincoat in the cloakroom before going to my desk. It was dark in there, and I always thought it was kind of spooky. I had to go all the way down to the end, where it was the darkest, to find a spot to hang my raincoat. I finally managed to grab a hanger, put my coat on it, and reached up to put it on the bar. As I did so, however, the bar collapsed, sending all the coats, hangers, and everything right down on top of me. It happened so fast I had no time to react. I was pinned down in the dark, unable to move.

In that moment, just as I was about to panic and start to cry and yell, that boy's words, *Don't worry, it will be all right*, came into my head. And so, I remained calm. The closet bar collapse had made a very loud noise, and it was not long before my teacher, Mrs. Burns, and several of my classmates started to remove the coats. I was able to get up a few minutes later and walked out on my own. Mrs. Burns commented on how brave I had been, and all thoughts of my being late for class were forgotten.

What I remembered, however, was how those words, uttered by a boy I had never seen before, were so timely as to what had happened.

A year later, there was another incident that began my lifetime of suspicion. I was now the proud owner of a new Schwinn bicycle. Sissy bars, orange banana seat, and chopper handlebars, it was my most valuable possession. I barely fit on the thing, but when spring came, I rode it every day.

My house featured a long straight driveway that, only at its end, dipped down to the garage door. Across the street and nearly in line was my neighbor's driveway. Even better, his driveway was ended on a hill leading straight off the street.

It didn't take long for me to come up with a new routine for my bike. I would start atop Mr. Hern's driveway. Check that the coast was clear of any cars traveling on the street. Then I would charge down the driveway, build up speed, zip across the street as I jogged a little to the right, and finally zoom down my own driveway. I would get as close to my garage door as possible before hitting the brakes. On a few occasions, I did crash into the garage door, but that was not totally unexpected.

What was unexpected was the one time I did this bike run and forgot to check the street first. On this occasion, as I left my neighbor's driveway and started across the street at full speed, I slammed into a moving car just as it crossed in front of me. My bike stopped, but I continued. I flew right over the hood of the car as it screeched to a halt and landed just where my driveway started. My dad happened to be painting the house at the time, witnessed what happened, and jumped about eight feet off the ladder before running up to me.

The driver got out of the car. She and my father reached me at about the same time.

Fortunately, I only suffered a bruised knee as my trip across the hood of the car used up most of my forward energy. But as my father and the lady driver started talking to each other, my eyes turned toward the passenger in the car. It was the same boy I had seen in school on that rainy day. He and I locked eyes for a moment, then my dad scooped me up and brought me into the house. The woman and boy drove off.

There was one more element to the story that I recalled only when I was telling my parents what happened. A split second before I started my bike run down the driveway, I thought I heard a young boy's voice said, "Wait." It caused me to hesitate for just a second. As it turned out, had I not gone through that false start, I would have arrived in the street a second or two sooner. And if that had happened, I would have been hit by the car instead of me hitting it. It was at this time that I made note of the coincidences that had occurred twice now involving that boy and events that turned out not as bad as they could have. But at eight years old, such thoughts soon faded away.

Fast forward two years. Now it is summer, and I am a ten-year-old camper at a private summer camp for children in north central New Jersey. The weather has been great, and among the many activities, it is the swim program I am most proud of. I had recently passed a swim test and was now allowed to swim out beyond the dock area to the raft, a floating platform about fifty yards further out on the lake. It was afternoon free swim, and I decided to go to the raft.

I swam out using the crawl stroke, the most common swimming technique. I would stop once in a while to tread water. This allowed me to get my bearing to the raft and stay on course. After a few cycles of this, I was getting a little tired, but since it was only a short distance further to the raft, I continued.

I swam and swam, expecting to hit the raft at any moment. After a while, I started to get a feeling that something was wrong. So once again, I went to treading water for a look around. It turned out that on my last swim cycle, I had overshot the raft and ended up much further out into the lake. The raft was now behind me, and it seemed quite a distance away. And by now, I was very tired. I had learned that in such an emergency to go to a back float to try to get some rest, but inside I was starting to get nervous.

After a few minutes on my back, I went again to treading water to locate the raft for a now desperate chance to swim to it. Suddenly, to my surprise, I saw a boy in a rowboat not ten feet away. It was not a camp boat as ours were square bowed skiff-type boats. This was a pointy bowed wooden rowboat, and I assumed the boy lived in one of the homes across the lake.

"Grab onto the boat, and I will take you to the raft," I heard the boy said.

That I did with what seemed to be the last of my strength. I was able to get some rest while being towed. After a few minutes, my ordeal was over. I released the boat, grabbed onto the ladder, and hauled myself up onto the raft. As I looked back, I saw the boy as he rowed away.

"Come back," I yelled because I wanted to thank him and talk to him.

"Can't," he replied. "Gotta go, see you around." He smiled and as he did so, recognition flooded my brain. It was him. My memories of this person came back in a rush. This event now rendered all beyond any realm of coincidence, and for the first time, I thought of this person, this boy just like me, as my guardian angel, a protector of some sort. Something very strange was going on, and my suspicions were once again aroused. But I could not find a rational explanation for what was happening.

During the next few years, as life went on, I only rarely thought of these events. It seemed too unbelievable to be true. And so, during my teen years, as similar episodes occurred, I just went with them, didn't challenge their reality or reason. I remember one time, when I was sixteen, I had an after-school job at a printing company. Among my tasks was to clean the excess ink off the print rollers on the enormous press machine as others were setting it up to do a press run; that is, to start printing the newspapers. The rag that was draped on my arm got caught in the rollers as the machine started up. I felt the tug, gentle at first, and realized my arm was being pulled into the rollers. The emergency stop button was out of range, and with such a high noise level, my yelling would not do much good.

Out of nowhere, a coworker appeared. He had a knife in his hand and used it to slash through the rag. I immediately shook the rag off my arm and ran over and pressed the stop button. By the time I looked back, my coworker, guess who, was already leaving the pressroom. After the initial shock of seeing my guardian again, I ended up giving him a silent thank you and got back to work.

That was but one example on how I decided to deal with this phenomenon. Trying to make sense of the situation had always been a frustrating exercise, and I did not want to obsess about it. Why me? How does he do it? What does it all mean? How does he know when to show up? Yes, there were many questions. And no answers. I made note of the fact that he never talked to me unless he had to and even then, only enough to get the business at hand completed—more of a bodyguard than a friend. But also, one who had saved my life on several occasions. Why? I recognized that I could lose my mind dwelling on such things, so for my own health decided to continue to just accept the situation, no questions asked.

As I went through adulthood, these interventions continued. Once, when my wife and I brought our two young children to an Arena Football game, we were able to purchase great seats, right up against the perimeter wall on the thirty-yard line. Real close to the action. At one point during the game, a voice behind me said, "Watch the quarterback." Rather than turn around to see who had spoken, I knew who it was. I did what he said. And, on the very next play, the quarterback overthrew the football, and it made a beeline directly at my head. But because I was paying attention, I was able to deflect the ball, no harm done.

A few years later, my brother and I went to build a tree stand in the woods of our hunting club property. I was towing a trailer with his off-road quad at the back. The plan was to pick up our supplies at a nearby home depot, drive my truck into the woods as far as possible, and tow the materials the rest of the way to the site with the quad. All went well until we went to take the quad off the trailer. The quad key was missing.

After an exhaustive search, we decided to drive my truck back to the store to see if anyone there had found it. But as helpful as they were, the store associates could not help us. As a last resort, my brother and I started searching the parking lot in case the key had been dropped out there.

As I crossed a lane in the parking lot, searching along the ground, a guy on a motorcycle pulled up ahead of me in the next lane and said, "Are you looking for this?" He was holding up what looked like a key. As I took a few steps toward him, now between two parked cars, I heard a roar behind me. A huge SUV came barreling down the lane I had just been in. It probably would have killed me had I not stepped forward at that moment. My guardian then put the key on top of one of the parked cars in his lane and drove off—his work done for the day. As freaked out as I was, I saw no reason to make a big deal of this to my brother but instead, shared in the joy of finding the quad key.

I never thought of myself as special. I never knew why I had a guardian angel. Oh, I had read all the journals and textbook definitions of guardian angels. How everyone had one or even more than one in some faiths, but I never saw any evidence of anyone else going through what I was going through. And I never tried to take advantage of the situation either, by taking unnecessary risks or attempting crazy stunts. Neither did I ever see anything about this situation that was supernatural. Until, that is, something happened later in my life.

This time, I was driving down a busy main street in town when I saw him. He was older as was I. The same face I had seen sporadically on and off all my life. Our eyes met very briefly as he sped past me in the fast lane.

Suddenly he cut me off, pulled out of the fast lane, and got right in front of me as we approached a red light. It made no sense, and I was just about to get out and approach his car when the light changed. But instead of taking off, his car seemed to stall. While he attempted to restart his car, I could hear those behind me honking their horns. However, I did not. I had been through too many experiences with this person to believe that this was a random event.

After about a minute, he finally was able to restart his car. By this time, the horn blowers had switched lanes and passed us, yelling as they did so. He started off at a slow pace, and I followed. At the next intersection, he turned left onto a side street. As tempted as I was to follow him and confront him, I did not as my destination was further down the road. I was very suspicious that something was about to happen, and tragically, I was right.

Ahead of me, a few hundred yards further down, was another traffic light. One of the drivers who had honked his horn was approaching the light at a high speed. He was clearly in a hurry and maybe still annoyed at being held up at the earlier light.

As the light ahead turned yellow and then red, the driver did not slow down but instead accelerated even faster to run the light. It was a fatal mistake. A gasoline tanker truck had just started to cross the intersection. The driver slammed into the truck at nearly eighty miles per hour. Though fuel trucks are built to withstand collisions, this was too much. There was only a brief second when I heard the screech of metal.

The following explosion was massive. Flames consumed the fuel truck. The car that hit it and at least two of the trailing cars were also completely engulfed in flames. I skidded to a stop. There was no way anyone in those cars ahead of me could have survived. Besides the flames, the shock of the explosion had deformed the cars, even tossing one upside down.

After taking in this terrible sight, my mind shifted to my own situation. I was all right. Not even slightly burned. All because I had chosen to stay behind my guardian angel when he stalled. If I hadn't done that, I would have been in one of the cars destroyed by the explosion.

With a sudden compulsion, I decided to change my strategy, to confront him once and for all. This, I thought, was the last straw. I did not want to let this one go. So I turned around and sped off, not to avoid the fire but to find my guardian. I got to the street I had seen him turn onto only minutes before. As I slowed down to carefully seek out his car, I could hear the first of the sirens of the emergency vehicles. I continued driving down the street for a few moments, and there, there was his car pulled over to the curb just ahead of me. And there he was, just walking down a driveway between two houses. I pulled over, slapped the gear shifter into park, and charged out of my car.

It was at this point that I saw something perhaps I should not have seen. Something that once again changed the narrative for me about this entire thing. I had turned off the street and started walking down the driveway. There was my guardian right in front of me about twenty yards away. He was walking straight to the garage, about ten more feet to go. He did not notice me behind him. He turned his head left and then right, I guess to see if there was anyone around.

Then he disappeared. He just vanished into thin air. I ran up to where I had seen him last. Did he go through a garage door? Suddenly bolt left or right as I blinked? I looked around. The garage door was securely closed. On both left and right, there was fence and a closed gate. As a result, I had no choice but to believe my eyes.

I ended up just going home afterward. My wife could see that I was bothered. When she asked me what was wrong, I told her about the accident, and of course, that was enough. But it missed the point entirely as to what was really wrong for me. I had never told my wife or anyone else for that matter, about my guardian angel. It seemed too bizarre a tale to be believed. So I kept things to myself and developed my own coping strategies, never seeking help in any way. And so now, when I felt that either I or the situation had crossed a line of sorts, I felt trapped for the first time. And it scared me.

But, as it turned out, my fear was not to last long.

A few months later, I had a mild heart attack and found myself in the hospital. It was a sudden onset, no warning, and much more painful than I ever imagined it would be. My doctors stabilized me, and I was scheduled for surgery a few days later to insert a couple of stents.

I was napping in my hospital bed the afternoon before the surgery, when I heard someone enter the room. He introduced himself as Dr. John Dominica. He was my anesthesiologist for the upcoming surgery and proceeded to walk me through the expected sequence of events. I was still a little bit fuzzy from my nap, and he had a surgical mask on his face. But as he was speaking, once again, recognition raised my eyebrows.

"I know who you are," I interrupted. "You are my guardian, my guardian angel." Part of me also recognized that the name he gave me was a combination of my fraternal grandparents' names. Coincidence? I didn't think so.

"I don't know what you are talking about," he responded, by way of evasion. But I was having none of that.

"Cut it out. I am as familiar with you as you are with me," I said. "We have been linked all our lives, and you are my protector. Don't deny it." I looked him directly in the eyes, even rising a bit off the bed.

His face changed—from one of a professional to one of a long-lost relative. He looked down for a moment and then back up, meeting my eyes.

Before he could respond, I jumped back in. "I assume you can't tell me much. I know you are more than a man, and I know you have some supernatural powers. Either that or I have lived a life as a crazy person. So which is it?"

"Well, Ted, you are not crazy. And yes, I am your guardian angel," he spoke low and slow." You are right about what you said. I can't tell you too much, but I am allowed to share a few things with you."

He continued, "We are linked, you and I, but in a way that is more than our lives. True, I am your guardian, but more importantly, I am the guardian of your soul."

"My soul?" I asked.

"That's right," he responded. "Humans are the only creatures to have a soul. Of all life on earth, we have been granted that special gift. That which links us to God. And, yes, Ted, there is a God up there," he chuckled. "And down there and all around actually. The forces of nature, the laws of physics, unconditional love, these are all of God. As is our intellect. As a species, we are the only ones granted the ability to self-reflect. How ironic it is that some use this gift to deny God.

So you see, the human soul must be looked after, protected, and continued throughout humanity. There is lot more to this than you can be told but suffice to say that we are bearers of the future of the human race. Any time a soul is corrupted, it is lost forever, never to be again passed to another person. And humanity, as a result, diminishes. We as protectors are tasked with trying to keep souls in our care worthy of continuity.

When your life ends, so will mine. But our souls will continue in new lives. The last thing I can tell you at this time is that in the next cycle, your soul is to be elevated to a guardian. It is a great honor for you, for both of us."

My guardian angel seemed to change once again, back to the professional. "That is all I have for you now, Ted. Get some rest, and I will see you tomorrow afternoon at the surgery."

Before I could stop him and ask him the first of about a million questions, he turned abruptly and left the room.

Here I am now, on surgery day. I have spent most of the morning chronicling as many events I could remember about the experiences I have had with my guardian angel. I am hoping to have more to add after the operation. As far as I know, there could be many others out there with similar situations, but this is an accounting in case this is a rare occurrence or, to be frank, in case I do not make it out of surgery. I know that sooner or later all will be revealed, but for now, I am satisfied as to finally understand why I have been granted the life I had.

About the Author

TED DELGROSSO IS A lifelong resident of northern New Jersey. In his youth, he was active in the Boy Scouts and in martial arts. He later did a four-year tour in the United States Navy as a hull technician, specializing in damage control. Following the Navy, he earned a bachelor's degree at Montclair State University and has been employed at The Home Depot for the last twenty-five years. He and his wife, Susan, have two grown children, David and Diana.

CPSIA information can be obtained
at www.ICGtesting.com
Printed in the USA
JSHW050005200922
30723JS00003B/14